"[BLACK MOON RISING] was holy wow."
  – Starswarlover (Reader, Amazon Kindle)

"Ann Simas has struck gold [with BURIED TO DIE). It's a great read."
  – Chuck Wallace, Reader (via Ann Simas Facebook page)

"I like everything about [FRUITYCAKES]. It gave me such a warm feeling and it also made me laugh."
  – Annette (Reader, BookBub)

"Loved HERE AND GONE. Couldn't hardly put it down, but my animals and husband needed to eat."
  – Nora Levenhagen (Paperback Reader, Amazon)

"[HERE AND GONE] just pulls you in and you just keep reading and reading to find out what happens next."
  – Jamie Kurp (via Candid Book Reviews)

"[HERE AND GONE] proves to be stuffed with danger and drama…[Ann Simas] has given her finest in this one keeping us engaged through every bit."
  – Denise Van Plew (Reader, Amazon Kindle)

"Death threats, crooked cops, sexual tension, dead bodies, crop circles, and a cliffhanger all wrapped up in a satisfying thriller [in QUILTED TO DIE]!"
  – Kindle Reader (Reader, Amazon Kindle)

"You may need tissues for [ANGELS ON THE ROOFTOP]."
  – Christine Campbell (Reader, Amazon Kindle)

"[DECK THE GNOMES] is a fun entertaining holiday romance that had me laughing out loud at times."
  – Brenda M. (Reader, Amazon Kindle)

"BACK-DOOR SANTA is such a cute and funny romance novel. [Simas] has a way with her characters that I never really see that much in other books."
  – Jessica Mitchell (Reader, Amazon Kindle)

"I am currently on my second reading of HELLFIRE. Excellent book!
  – lfb68 (Reader, Amazon Kindle)

"I loved, loved, loved [TAKEN TO DIE]! It took me a month to get started reading this book because I knew I wouldn't want it to end. I love the Grace Gabbiano series so much and can hardly wait for the next installment."
  – cocogib (Reader, Amazon Kindle)

Books by Ann Simas...

Afterstories
Chloe's Spirit[†]
Chloe's Spirit Afterstories
First Star[†]
First Star Afterstories

Stand-Alones
Blessed Are the Eagles[†]
Loose Ends
Heaven Sent
Black Moon Rising
Here and Gone

Grace Gabbiano Mysteries
Dressed to Die
Sliced to Die
Buried to Die
Quilted to Die
Taken To Die
Praying to Die *(coming July 2020)*

Andi Comstock Supernatural Mysteries
Holy Smoke
Penitence
Angel Babies
Hellfire
The Wrong Wicca *(coming Fall 2020)*

Christmas Valley Romances
Santa's Helper
Candy Cane Lane
Let It Snow
FruityCakes
Sleigh Bride
Angels on the Rooftop
Deck the Gnomes
Back-Door Santa
Jingle Bell Clock
Reindeer Blitz

Short Story Collection
All's Well

[†]RWA Golden Heart Finalists

Jingle Bell Clock

Ann Simas

MAGIC
MOON
PRESS

JINGLE BELL CLOCK

November 2019

ISBN 978-0-9993858-8-3 (print book)

Magic Moon Press . POB 41634 . Eugene, OR 97404-0386

Editing by Nancy Jankow

Printed in U.S.A.
120119/11.5pthyph
KP 999385883

This book is for
everyone who believes
in the magic of
Christmas

Don't watch the clock;
do what it does.

Keep going.
— Sam Levenson

Chapter 1

Tally Barrow awoke to a room cloaked in darkness. If not for one small nightlight—a flickering bubble candle—she wouldn't have been able to see anything.

From the sounds of things outside, Old Man Winter was having a heyday with the weather. The screeching of bare branches against her bedroom window amplified his tantrum, but she didn't mind the scratchy sound. In fact, it comforted her in a way she couldn't define. She closed her eyes, content to be tucked safe in her bed.

Her thoughts came slowly, as if her brain deliberately held them back. She opened her eyes again and stared at the candle nightlight, searching her memory for why it seemed out of place. Nothing came to her and, finally, her eyes drifted closed and she gave into sleep.

The next time she woke, the room was still dark, informing her that dawn hadn't yet broken. The candle nightlight continued to cast a subtle glow over her surrounds, which made the room she'd last decorated as a teenager dance with shadows.

That's when it occurred to Tally something was wrong.

She had the strangest feeling she wasn't a teenager any longer.

In fact, she was sure she was a grown woman. She had no idea why she was so certain of that, but she knew that she hadn't slept in this bedroom for almost ten years.

Rather than lie there and stew about how she'd come to be back in her old bedroom, she decided to get up and check things out.

She lifted her arm to throw back the covers, but it felt as if it were weighted down with a hundred-pound dumbbell. Still, she didn't give up. Eventually, she managed to free herself from the tangle of sheets and blankets, but something still constrained her arm.

Exhausted by that little bit of exertion, she opted to rest for a few minutes. While she did that, she pondered why she'd conjured up the word *free* in terms of the bedcovers. It wasn't like she was being held prisoner in a gulag somewhere.

With no plausible explanation presenting itself, she gave up thinking about it and turned her attention back to the candle nightlight.

Fascinated by the bubbles burbling inside the glass tube, she couldn't tear her eyes away. She'd loved that Christmas night light as a child, but now…. She shuddered.

Confused, because she had a vague memory of loving everything Christmas, she couldn't figure out why she now seemed to find the holiday repugnant.

She pushed herself to a sitting position, surprised when the small effort wore her out. Not only was her arm constrained, but there was something between her legs, too. Something not comfortable at all. What was going on?

Little by little, she slid her legs over the side of the bed. Her dangling toes brushed against something that wasn't the carpet she remembered covering the floor. She shook her arm, attempting to free it from whatever had her in its grasp.

A shimmer of fear seized her. Was she having a dream? Or worse, was she in the middle of a waking nightmare? Would the maniacal clown from *Poltergeist* pop out from beneath the bed at any moment?

Her eyes wandered around the shadowy room. It was her bedroom, but not her bedroom. As a teenager, she'd had a twin bed, but the bed on which she sat now had four posters, and it was much larger than her twin bed.

The curtains at the window were gone, and in their place, wide-slat blinds shut out the angry night. A fabric swag flanked each side of the window. Her old dresser was gone, as well, replaced by an antique armoire. She searched for other changes. No shelves to hold stuffed animals and books. No beanbag chair to flop down into. Instead, a club chair had taken its place.

She fumbled with the switch of the lamp on the bedside table. The bright light temporarily blinded her.

Tally shut her eyes for a moment, then opened them to slits, and finally, all the way.

Shock washed through her. With it came reality, and a small bit of clarity. Memories hurled through her mind. Startling memories. Memories that had the power to level her.

She switched off the lamp in hopes of hiding from those memories and crawled back under the covers. She curled into a fetal position, uncomfortable as all get-out, but determined to turn off the memories threatening to overcome her.

Was she dead? Could you feel physical pain and mental anguish in death?

Rather than deal with those questions, Tally succumbed to the call of a deep sleep that was anything but welcoming.

Chapter 2

A noise roused Tally from sleep. Still curled into a ball, she'd cried herself to sleep, but now she was on her back again. Eyes still closed, she mewled a sound of discomfort.

"Every time she does that, I think she's coming out of the coma," said Jean Barrow, her mother.

"Me, too," her father, Bryan, agreed. "Maybe one of these days when she moans, it will mean something."

"I pray that's true."

The quiet shuffle of footsteps mingled with the echo of their sad voices. A moment later, the door closed softly and they were gone.

Tally's eyelids inched open. The room was empty and the blinds had been opened to reveal the sunny, winter wonderland outside.

No wonder she recognized the bedroom. She'd rented this apartment exactly because the bedroom was so similar to the one she'd grown up in. She had a view of the snowy hills and room enough for the four-poster bed she'd always dreamed of owning. Hardwood floors ran throughout the apartment, scattered here and there with rugs. She also had a walk-in closet that she would have killed for as a teenager. As a grown woman, not even half the storage area was taken up by clothes and shoes. The remainder held the beloved Christmas decorations and memorabilia she'd collected over the years.

In the light of day, she seemed to have more energy. She tossed back the covers and sat up, staring in consternation at the IV attached to her arm. For a moment, it befuddled her as she attempted to get a grip on the foggy memories still swimming inside her head.

In the end, all she knew was that something must have happened to her. Something bad. Something that had resulted in her needing an IV, even though she was at home, in her own bed.

Her next realization was that the IV had to go.

Inch-by-inch, she peeled away the tape holding the needle in place, then with one swift yank, she pulled it out of her arm and let it drop to the floor. She remembered from a previous blood draw that it was important to apply pressure to the spot. She grabbed a tissue from the box on the bedside table and pressed it against the wound to staunch the blood that came immediately to the surface. Since she had no tape to secure the tissue in place, she pressed her thumb against it, simultaneously glancing at the bedside clock. Five minutes. She'd apply pressure for five minutes.

That gave her time to think about why she felt discomfort between her legs. When it hit her, she let out a little squeak.

Once the five minutes was up, she lifted the tissue. No more blood. She tossed it onto the nightstand and tugged at her nightgown, revealing a tube as she raised the fabric. She debated whether or not to call her parents back, then decided she could remove the catheter herself. Inch by tortuous inch, she worked the tube out, grateful it wasn't full. That reminded her that the IV fluid was probably leaking out onto the hardwood floor. A glance down confirmed it.

She climbed out of bed without much effort and wobbled over to retrieve the wastebasket beside the armoire. Backtracking her steps, she picked up both the IV needle and the catheter and dropped them into the container before she made her way to the window in slow, but slightly steadier steps. Old Man Winter's storm had left a good foot of snow in its wake.

Tally longed to get dressed and run outside to make a snow angel. And maybe after that, have a snowball fight with the neighborhood kids. She'd lucked out finding this apartment in a nice neighborhood peppered with youngsters who still liked to play outdoors. They always loved pelting her with snowballs, and vice versa.

When she finally turned to look at the clock, she discovered ten minutes had passed. For the first time, she noticed that both the head and foot of her bed were elevated. She ventured back to the bed and picked up the remote on the bedside table. At the push of a button, the head of the bed went down, then the foot of the bed. She pressed the button labeled 1 and watched in amazement as both the head and the foot rose to the previous position. She had no memory of purchasing a mattress that had the capability of raising and lowering.

Tally studied the room again. An IV pole stood beside the bed, along with a collection bag for the catheter. A blood pressure cuff had been placed in a small basket on the bedside table. It also contained a thermometer, a heating pad, and various other medical supplies.

She turned away from the bed and crossed to her closet. Her hand hovered near the pocket door latch for several moments before she slid it open. She turned on the light and stepped inside.

White banker's boxes lined six of the shelves. Tally frowned. The last thing she wanted around her was anything related to Christmas, but for the life of her, she couldn't remember why.

Feeling angry all of a sudden, she backed out of the closet and went to the ensuite bathroom. For some reason, she felt like she hadn't taken a shower in a long while.

Maybe having one would wash her anger down the drain.

From the bathroom doorway, she turned and studied her bed again. An IV, a catheter, a mattress that raised and lowered. Why had she needed all of that?

No ready answer came to her.

She turned and entered the bathroom, stopping in front of the mirror over the vanity. She stared at her reflection in horror. Her hair was at least six inches longer than she remembered. How was that even possible?

She grabbed hold of the countertop to steady herself. Was she still experiencing the living nightmare she'd awoken to earlier?

She contemplated that question for several minutes. This was too real to be a dream, or a nightmare. She grabbed her toothbrush and set about brushing her teeth, certain she wouldn't have been able to taste the minty flavor of toothpaste in a dream.

That done, she stripped, letting her nightgown lay where it fell, and reached in to turn on the shower faucet. While she waited for the water to heat up, she used the toilet, then stepped into the oversized stall.

No dream had ever felt this good. This was real life, with real warm water, real shampoo, and real soap suds lathering her skin. Once she'd finished, she stepped out onto the bath mat to dry, studying her reflection in the mirror once more. Unable to see her entire body, except from her belly button up, she shut the bathroom door to access the full-length mirror on the back side.

My God...she'd not only grown six inches of hair overnight, but she'd lost at least ten pounds. She didn't find her new form unappealing, but she did find it confusing. No one could lose that much weight overnight.

She hung up the towel and picked up her nightie. It dawned on her that she didn't recognize it.

From the time she'd been a toddler, when she'd first been allowed to spend the night at Granny Marigold's house, her grandmother had gifted her with several pairs of pajamas, all in festive colors and prints. Tally had loved them because they matched the ones Granny Marigold had made for herself.

Tally's heart clenched. Her beloved grandmother had died while she was in high school. She missed her like crazy, but she was thankful for the special memories the two of them had made together. To this day, she was a pajama girl, but she understood she couldn't have had a catheter while wearing PJs, which explained the nightgown.

Back in the closet, she pulled open the top built-in drawer and withdrew her underwear, including socks, then slipped into a pair of jeans and a sweatshirt. The denim that had hugged her body tightly before, didn't now, and the zipper closed with ease. When she realized the sweatshirt was decorated with a blinking-nose Rudolph, she ripped it off and dug deeper until she found one that said JUST DO IT beneath the Nike Swoosh. She shoved her feet into loafers, then went back to the bathroom to blow-dry her hair. By the time she was done, she realized she actually liked the longer length, but it still puzzled her that it had grown so quickly.

With a shrug, she put away the dryer and left the bathroom.

The scent of freshly brewed coffee assailed her as soon as she pulled open the bedroom door. She slowly made her way to the kitchen, dying for a cup of coffee.

Her parents, her brother Micah, and a man she didn't recognize, carried on a conversation at the kitchen table in hushed tones.

"Good morning," she said.

Four heads whipped around in her direction. All wore shocked expressions.

"Tally!" her mother cried. She pushed away from the table so hard, her chair fell backward and hit the floor.

Her father echoed her mother's cry, as did Micah. The stranger merely stared at her in shock.

Frightened by their reactions, Tally took a step back.

Jean threw her arms around her, sobbing, holding on so

tight Tally almost couldn't breathe. "Mom, what's got into you?"

Her dad came to such an abrupt halt, Micah bumped into his back.

"What's wrong with all of you?" Tally asked.

"Don't you remember?" Micah asked.

"Remember what?"

"The accident?"

"Accident? What accident?"

When no one else answered, the stranger spoke up. "The car crash, Tally. You were hit by a drunk driver."

She tilted her head at him, frowning. "Who are you?" By his crestfallen expression, she presumed she should have known him, but try as she might, she couldn't conjure up more than a hazy memory of him.

"Sam Reed," he said, his voice rough with emotion. When she didn't respond, he said, "I'm a firefighter," as if that would explain everything.

Micah backtracked to the table and placed a hand on Sam-the-firefighter's shoulder. "Hold on, man."

Sam nodded.

Bryan took two steps forward and wrapped his arms around his wife and daughter. Tears ran down his cheeks unchecked. "Thank God, Tally."

"Thank God for what?" she asked.

"Thank God you're alive and you're…okay."

Okay being the relative term, Tally supposed, since she didn't remember the incident. "When was the crash?" she asked for lack of a better question. All that clarity she thought she'd achieved just a short while earlier was out the window.

Dead silence met her query.

Her parents glanced at Micah, who looked at the firefighter, Sam Somebody-or-other. She assumed that since he was the only one in the room with medical training, they expected him to answer her question. Maybe he'd been one of the first responders at the crash.

"December," he said just before he tore his gaze away

from her. "I should go and give you guys your family time." He stood and pulled his jacket from the back of the chair he'd occupied, tugging it on.

Why was everyone acting so wiggy? Tally searched each face, but their expressions revealed no answers, only more questions.

On his way to the front door, the firefighter stopped. "I'm really glad you're awake, Tally. A lot of people have been worried about you."

She squirmed in her parent's embrace to face him, but he walked out of her apartment without a backward glance. When she turned back to her parents, she asked, "What's wrong with him?"

"He's been waiting so patiently," her mother said, sniffling.

"Patiently for what?"

"You."

"Me? But I don't even know him."

"Let's sit down," Tally's father said. "I think some explanations are in order."

"Should I call the doctor?" Micah asked.

"Yes," both her parents said at the same time.

Micah nodded and pulled out his phone. "Hey, Doc, she's awake. ... I understand. ... Okay, see you when you get here."

Sam Reed climbed into his double-cab Tundra, unable to put the key in the ignition, or even move. He'd been waiting almost a year for Tally to come out of the coma and this was how it ended? She not only didn't recognize him, she apparently had no memory of him whatsoever.

He'd battled his fears over the past eleven months. Fear that she'd never come out of the coma. Fear that when she did, she'd have brain damage. Fear that she'd have such a drastic personality change, it would affect her and everyone around her in a negative way. He'd never contemplated that she wouldn't recognize him, or remember the sparks flowing between them for the three short days they'd had together before the crash.

Sean D'Arcy rolled by on the road running past Tally's apartment in a D'Arcy Implements tractor. A snow plow was attached to the front of it. Sean waved at him and he waved back. At least something in life was still normal.

A few minutes later, Fergus Sullivan pulled into the vacant parking spot next to him. Sam climbed out of his truck. For whatever good it would do, he needed to talk to the doctor.

"I hear she's awake," Fergus said.

Sam nodded, but couldn't speak.

"What's wrong?"

"She doesn't remember the crash...or me."

"Amnesia and comas are funny ailments, Sam."

"I'm not laughing."

"Neither am I, and I certainly wasn't using the word *funny* in any comedic sense. Medical experts can define amnesia and comas and tell you what to expect, but there are times when it's not like that at all." He put a hand on Sam's shoulder. "Basically, any prognosis with head trauma is a crap shoot. You have to be patient, son."

Sam glanced away, blowing out his frustration in a breath that left a visible plume in front of his face. "I've *been* patient."

"I can't argue that, but you have to be patient a little longer. Amnesia is like one of the fires you put out, Sam. It might start out in nightmarish proportions, but as a firefighter, you know if you persevere, you'll put it out."

Sam's agonized gaze turned back to the doctor. "If you could've see the way she looked at me a few minutes ago, you wouldn't be trying to cheer me up. You'd know it's over before it ever got started."

"Things will change, you'll see." Fergus studied him for a moment. "Why don't you join me and Franny for dinner tonight? My place, around six?"

Sam considered declining. He wasn't in any mood to be

social at the moment, but by dinnertime, Doc Sullivan would have more of a big-picture perspective about Tally's condition. By evening, he'd also be drowning in his need to know more. *Admit it, you're already starved for more information about her.* "Thanks, I'd like that. Can I bring anything?"

"Just yourself."

Sam nodded and went back to his truck. He could almost feel Doc Sullivan's gaze showering pity on him for being nothing but a lovesick fool.

Chapter 3

Tally sank down into the chair she usually sat in to eat her solitary meals, a frown firmly in place. "I don't see why you have to call the doctor just because I woke up this morning."

Micah took the seat Sam had vacated. Jean and Bryan claimed the two chairs on either side of her. They each grasped one of her hands.

"Tally, baby," her father began. "The car crash was in December…and this is November. Thanksgiving was last Thursday."

She laughed, amused, but none of them cracked a smile, or chuckled at his joke. "Very funny, Dad."

Her father shared a worried glance with her mother.

"You're serious," Tally said after a moment.

Her father nodded.

"But…." She found herself at a loss for words.

Her mother didn't have the same problem. "You were headed to work at Gingerbread Cottage when you were hit head-on by a drunk driver. He and his passenger were both killed when they veered off the road and crashed into the electrical substation."

Stunned, Tally could only think to ask, "Who was it?"

"Jim Fridley and his girlfriend."

"But…Jim is married to Lily's friend, Jani."

"At the time of the accident, they were in the middle of a divorce," her brother said.

"But…he was cheating on Jani?" she asked, incredulous. Jani Fridley had smarts, looks, a sense of humor, and a wardrobe to die for. Why would Jim cheat on her?

Her brother nodded.

"I don't get it. Jim always seemed like such a nice guy." She couldn't quite wrap her head around what they were saying. "Why was he drinking and driving? And why was he cheating on Jani?"

Her parents and her brother exchanged a glance, as if they were silently asking each other, *How much can she handle right off the bat?*

"Please, just spit it out!"

"He changed," Micah said.

"People change clothes, not personalities. What happened between them? They always seemed so happy together."

"It had to do with Jani wanting kids and Jim not wanting kids," Micah said.

"But…" She struggled to grasp a memory. "I remember Jani telling me they were trying to get pregnant."

"He may have been an active participant" —her brother shrugged— "but maybe he was shooting blanks."

"Either way, Jani found out he had a girlfriend," her mother inserted.

That irked Tally to no end. "He should have got a divorce first, then started screwing around. What kind of man does that to his wife?"

"The kind who's a jerk," her father said.

Jean nodded her agreement.

"What an asshole," Tally said, shocking her parents.

"You get no argument from me on that, sis," Micah said, "but watch your mouth, okay?"

A knock sounded at the door. "I'll get it," Jean said. She returned moments later with Fergus Sullivan, a retired orthopedic surgeon, who had moved to Christmas Valley to be closer to his daughter, Esme O'Donnell, and his grandson, Arran.

Fergus smiled at Tally as he removed his coat and handed it to Jean. "You look amazingly like you haven't gone through hell for the last eleven months."

"What do you mean?" Tally asked, her eyes wide. "What kind of hell?"

"You had several broken bones, in addition to head trauma. I treated the orthopedic end of your injuries."

"Who treated my head trauma?" She glanced at her mother, then back at the doctor. "Why can't I remember anything? Do I have amnesia?"

"It would appear so, Tally," he said in a gentle voice, "but it's nothing to be alarmed about. Greyson Dixon, the neurologist who looked after you for the injury to your brain, is tops in his field."

Learning that she was missing not only months of her life, but memories of the events leading up to those missing months, scared the crap out of her. "Will my memory come back?"

"We don't know that yet, but perhaps Grey can give you a better idea of what to expect."

Coupled with the shock her family and Sam What's-his-name had expressed, Tally read between the lines of the doctor's comments and came up with her own interpretation. No one had been sure her brain would survive the ordeal of the crash, if she ever fully woke again. The only thing she could think to say was, "I don't like having missing pieces in my life."

"No one would," Fergus assured her, taking the chair Bryan offered him.

"I don't remember the accident at all." She paused. "Or working at Gingerbread Cottage, for that matter. What about my job at Tidwell's?"

Bryan said, "They downsized and cut your hours."

Jean added, "You were supplementing your income at the Cottage."

"That doesn't sound like me. I don't even like Christmas anymore."

"It sounds exactly like you," her mother said, her voice laced with concern. "Sylvie was giving you pointers and Bonnie and the FruityCakes owners were impressed with your ability to merchandise and increase sales."

"They were?"

"Yeah," Micah said. He glanced at his parents, then added, "You hired Sylvie to decorate my house for Christmas, remember?"

Tally stood and moved over to the counter, where she stared out the kitchen window at the snow. She hated Christmas, didn't she? Why the heck would she ever work in a Christmas store, or hire Sylvie to decorate her brother's house for Christmas? Why couldn't she remember any of what they were telling her?

While Doc Sullivan checked Tally's vitals, Micah went to the other room to call his wife. "Sylvie, she's awake!"

"Oh, thank God!" Sylvie said, and promptly burst into tears.

"Fergus is checking her over now, then he's going to give her a lift over to the hospital to see the neurologist."

"Does she have brain damage?" Sylvie asked.

"No, but she does have amnesia. She can't remember the crash, or working at Gingerbread Cottage, or hiring you to decorate my house." He took a deep breath. "She said she hates Christmas."

"That doesn't sound like her at all!"

"She can't remember Sam, either."

"Oh, no! How's he taking it?"

"Not well. When she didn't recognize him, he got up and left...not in a mad kind of way, though. I don't remember ever seeing a guy so dejected since you walked out on me before we were married."

"That worked out okay, didn't it?"

"Yeah, but it was hell on me for three agonizing days."

"I had some thinking to do."

"I know, babe, but at least you knew who I was. Tally seriously doesn't have any recollection of Sam."

"If they're meant to be together, she'll fall for him again."

Micah loved Sylvia like crazy, but no matter how much he wished it otherwise, he didn't have her confidence in matters of the heart, except where she was concerned.

As if she could hear his thoughts over the phone, she said, "This is Christmas Valley, remember? You have to keep the faith."

Micah knew that without Sylvie, he'd probably be lost, so who was he to doubt her? "I'll be home soon."

"Good, 'cuz Logan just told me he wants his daddy."

Micah laughed, then lowered his voice. "After lunch, when he goes down for his nap, I'll show you how much I want his mommy."

Sylvie practically purred. "I can hardly wait. Love you."

"Love you, too." He disconnected and headed back to the kitchen.

Tally went off to her bedroom to find her snow boots and her winter outerwear.

Jean fretted in the kitchen, pacing back and forth. "Are you sure she's well enough to go out in this weather, Fergus?"

"Her vitals are excellent and she has cold-weather gear to bundle up in. She'll be fine." The doctor packed up his bag and latched it. "If you're worried about her riding with me, she can hitch a ride in Micah's truck." He glanced at Micah and said, "We know he can navigate the snowy roads around here."

"I can," Micah shot back, "but Sean should be coming by any minute, doing the other side of the road." He glanced at his mother. "Would you feel better if he took her over to the hospital in the snowplow?"

"No, I know she'll be fine with you or Fergus." Jean wrung her hands. "I don't know what's wrong with me. I'm so relieved Tally's awake, but I feel like something's wrong."

Micah said, "It's partly because she says she doesn't like Christmas anymore."

"Oh, my goodness, you're right!"

Bryan slid an arm over his wife's shoulders. "Something else is wrong, too, honey. Tally doesn't have her memory back, and that's worrisome, but let's wait and see what the neurologist says before we freak out, okay?"

Jean nodded, but tears slipped down her cheeks. "I wish I wasn't such a worrier."

"Mom, *some*one has to be the designated family worrier," Micah teased.

"You're a fine one to talk!" she retorted.

"I know, but I turned out okay, didn't I?"

"You turned out way better than okay, and if you ever doubt that, all you have to do is look at Sylvie and that beautiful little boy the two of you made together."

Bryan hugged her. "So, we're agreed? No more worrying unless we have to, okay?"

"You're right." She swiped at her tears. "If Tally feels up to it, let's have a family dinner tonight."

"*If* she feels up to it," her husband agreed. "I wonder if we should invite Sam."

"Don't worry about Sam," Fergus said, pulling on his coat. "I ran into him in the parking lot and invited him to have dinner with me and Franny." He grinned. "I neglected to mention that Livvy will also be there."

"You naughty boy!" Jean said.

Livvy was Olivia Strangewayes when she was working as a psychic, or just plain Livvy O'Donnell, when she wasn't, and his daughter Esme's mother-in-law. Fergus shrugged. "I figured it couldn't hurt to have a little psychic intervention."

"I don't know how Livvy does it," Bryan said. "If I had psychic abilities, I'd probably disappear and live like a hermit in the woods."

Jean grinned and biffed his arm. "I thought you didn't even believe in psychic ability."

"I'm ambivalent about it," he informed her. "That's different."

Micah said, "I asked Murph about it once. He said his mother has no control over what comes to her, and if she can share the knowledge and make someone's life better, then that's what she does."

"She's an amazing woman." Fergus buttoned up his coat.

"Thanks for coming over so quickly," Jean said, hugging him.

"You're welcome."

Bryan and Micah shook his hand.

"We never stop worrying about our kids, do we?" he asked when he reached the front door.

The Barrows looked at him and said in unison, "Never."

Micah helped Tally climb into his truck, though she didn't know why he thought she needed any assistance.

"Thank you," she said politely.

He gave her a squinty-eyed look in response. "You okay?"

"I'm perfectly fine, except for not having my memories intact."

He studied her a moment more, then slammed the door shut and went around to the driver's side.

"Tell me what's been going on," she said as soon as he opened his door.

"You mean with the world, or with you?" he asked, buckling himself in. He glanced pointedly at her seatbelt until she did the same.

"Let's start small and deal with me. How long have I

really been in a coma, and how long have I been at home in my own bed?"

"You've really been in a coma since last December," he said. He turned the key and the engine roared to life. "You've been at home in your own bed since March."

"March," she said, stunned. "And this is November?"

"The thirtieth, to be exact. As Dad said, Thanksgiving was two days ago."

"So this is Saturday." She glanced over at him. "I bet the neurologist was thrilled to be called in on the weekend," she said, her tone droll.

"Actually, Grey asked us to contact him any time, day or night, when you came around."

"You're on a first-name basis with him?"

"I knew him from the Corps. We both left about the same time."

"I hope he's not as stuffy in person as his name implies."

"Cut him some slack, Tally. He'd just finished his residency when he decided he wanted to give back to his country, so he joined the Corps and spent five years in the Middle East treating soldiers. His neurology specialty came in handy so many times, I can't even tell you."

Tally had a million questions about that, but held them for later. "How is it that I was allowed to go home while I was in a coma?"

Micah checked for traffic, which was nonexistent on this particular Saturday because of the snowfall, and pulled out onto the main road. "It was a family decision, and one we agonized over for a week before we arrived at a consensus."

Her brother sounded exactly like the CFO he was of Barrow Logistics and Marketing. "So, Derek, Tessa, and Jennie were involved, too?"

He nodded. "Tessa and Jennie moved back here after your accident."

Shocked, Tally didn't know what to say. As the baby of the family at age twenty-eight—well, twenty-nine now and soon to be thirty—everyone always treated her as if she hadn't yet found her way in the world and they all had. Why would her sisters give up lucrative careers to come back to Christmas Valley? She asked as much.

"You're kidding, right?"

"No, I'm not. Tessa and Jennie both loved their jobs, and as I recall, they were thrilled when they ran away from home, so to speak."

"Things change," Micah said. "They're both more grown up now…maybe almost as much as you."

Tally barked out a laugh. "That's rich! How many times did all of you give me advice on how to live my life?"

He gave her a look. "I never once gave you any advice about anything, except when you told me you were hot for that douche bag in your building."

Tally conceded that with a nod. The one time she'd gotten serious over a guy, he'd turned out to be a loser.

"Back to your original question, we decided you'd heal faster at home than in a convalescent center, where they only cared for you because it was their job. Fergus was on board with it, but Grey took a little extra convincing."

"I still think he sounds pompous," she said, shooting him a grin to let him know she was half-teasing.

"And I still think you're incorrigible."

"Go on. I was allowed to go home to recover?"

"We organized a Tally Brigade. You have a lot of friends and they all agreed to chip in to help. With that kind of assistance, we created a calendar to organize sign-ups and off we went."

"Sign-ups for what?"

"Exercising you. The only way Fergus *and* Grey would consent is if you had someone moving your arms and legs and rolling you over so you wouldn't get bedsores, et cetera."

That gave Tally pause. "And these were all people I knew?"

He nodded. "For instance, when Bonnie came to exercise your arms and legs, Griff would accompany her so he could do the heavy lifting to turn you over, or sit you up, or whatever."

Tally had to think a moment. "Bonnie Hall. She was Joss's neighbor in the duplex, right?"

He nodded again. "She manages Gingerbread Cottage for Charley and Stevie and she hired you to work there."

Tally shivered.

"You cold?"

"A bit," she lied, though she wasn't sure why she didn't want her brother to know it was the mention of the Gingerbread Cottage that set her teeth on edge. Was it because she'd been on her way to work there when the crash happened?

He turned the heat up two degrees.

"And who is Griff?"

"An old friend of Tate's, who came to visit. Do you remember Tate, Charley's husband?"

"Yes, or at least, I think so. That memory is still a little fuzzy."

"Everyone got really good at exercising you, though at night, we had a different system in place."

"Like what?"

"For starters, we had trained health professionals in from the hospital, Monday through Friday. They were people who knew you from school or wherever, and wanted to supplement their income for whatever reason. On the weekends, Mom and Dad, Grandma and Grandpa, Sean's folks, Fergus, Livvy, Granny, G'ma, the Kringles, Coop's aunts and uncles, and so many others who didn't have Saturday-Sunday plans alternated weekends to take the night shifts."

Tally, who couldn't remember ever being floored about anything, stared at her brother in shocked silence. Tears rolled down her cheeks. "All those people?" she whispered.

"And more. You're a person everyone loves, Tally."

A mental image of the firefighter popped into her head. "What about the guy this morning?"

"What about him?"

"Was he one of the people who helped?"

"Yes."

Micah's simple answer raised even more questions in Tally's mind.

Chapter 4

Greyson Dixon, M.D., wasn't nearly as pompous as Tally had expected. In fact, he was down to earth and friendly. When he hugged her and said, "Welcome back to the living, Tally," she almost bawled again.

"Should I wait out here?" Micah asked.

"No, you can come back with us. Fergus gave me an update on his exam and I'm expecting this to be quick and painless." Grey flashed Tally an encouraging smile. "I'd say you're one for the record books, young lady."

"I never imagined myself setting any records."

Dr. Dixon grinned. "There's a first time for everything."

They followed him down the hallway to an exam room. Tally was surprised to see Sam What's-his-name sitting in the neurologist's office as they passed by. She stopped and stared at him. "Are you following us?"

Micah said, "It's obvious Sam was already here, so it's more likely we're following him."

Sam went for a smile and failed. "Grey and I are friends."

His expression was so somber, it disturbed her, and after that, she experienced a wave of guilt for her rudeness.

That was so not her, but for some reason, the firefighter seemed to have an adverse effect on her. Her gaze shot to the doctor, who nodded, as if to confirm Sam's statement, then back to the man in the chair, nursing a cup of coffee. "Did you rush right over here to tell him I'd come out of the coma?"

"Tally!" her brother said, his tone censuring.

Sam's expression didn't alter. "I'm here because Grey and I usually get together for coffee on Saturday mornings, if he's working and I'm not. If neither of us is working, we go skiing or horseback riding or do something else outdoors."

"How do you know each other?"

"We met in the military."

As if sensing a battle might be brewing, the doctor said, "Let's get that examination going, shall we?" He glanced at Sam. "We'll pick this up later. I'll give you a call."

Sam stood, nodding, but his eyes tracked back to Tally and lingered there.

She squirmed under his intense gaze, then moved away without another word.

"Sorry, Sam," she heard her brother say as she stalked off. "I don't know what's got into her. She's not usually this...."

"Hostile?" Sam filled in when her brother couldn't seem to come up with the proper word.

Tally could envision her brother nodding.

She resisted the urge to look over her shoulder. The last thing she wanted to see again was that expression on the firefighter's face. She may have been in a coma for the better part of a year, but she could read longing and regret in a person's eyes when she saw it.

Once Grey Dixon concluded his exam and the few tests he put to her, Tally found herself exhausted. She asked Micah to take her straight home.

"You sure? Sylvie and Logan would really like to see you."

"Maybe tomorrow."

"Mom and Dad went grocery shopping for you."

"That was nice of them."

"Can I ask you a question?"

"Yes, but I may not answer it."

He tore his gaze from the road to study her for a moment. "What have you got against Sam?"

"Nothing. I don't even know him."

"Technically, I suppose that's true."

"What's that supposed to mean?" When he didn't respond, she persisted. "Micah, don't play games with me. Is he a former boyfriend I don't remember, or something?"

"Not really."

She blew out an impatient breath.

"What I mean is, you met him when you were working at Gingerbread Cottage. He stopped in to see Bonnie and the way she tells it, you fell head-over-heels for him immediately."

"That's not possible," she shot back.

"Since you have no memory of him, or working at the Cottage, I hardly think you're in a position to say it's not possible."

Tally bit her tongue to keep from speaking as she considered her brother's words. Micah had never taken that tone with her before, and it surprised her. The more she thought about it, the more she knew he was right. How could she be so critical of someone or something she couldn't even remember? "I'm sorry."

"I'm not the one you should be apologizing to."

"I'm not apologizing to someone I can't remember." After a few moments that felt extremely tense, she asked, "How long did we date?"

"You knew him for three days before the accident." He shot her another look. "Since then, he's looked in on you every day that he's not working."

"He has? That sounds more like stalking to me."

Micah unexpectedly turned into the next parking lot, which happened to be a gas station. He shoved the gear into PARK and turned to her. "What's gotten into you?"

"What do you mean?"

"I mean, why are you acting like this about Sam? He's a great guy."

"I suppose I'll have to take your word for it."

"See? It's not like you to be so nasty."

"I wasn't being nasty, I was simply stating a fact." She turned to look out the window, hoping to hide her expression. "Why do you think he's a great guy?"

Micah sighed with impatience. "For one thing, he's a firefighter, and I have the utmost respect for his profession."

"His profession and his personal life are two different things."

"Granted, but when the duplex Joss and Bonnie lived in caught fire, Sam hauled ass and got people to open stores for him so he could buy all of them, including Bonnie's girls, something to wear, and he paid for it out of his own pocket."

She looked back at him.

Micah went on. "He did that without broadcasting it to the world."

"So how do you know, then?"

"Myrna told me."

"Myrna? The manager of The Emporium?"

"One and the same. Apparently, he's a regular customer when someone's house burns up with all their clothes in it."

"That was nice of him, I guess." She aimed her eyes back out the window.

Micah blew out a frustrated breath. "Myrna gives him a discount, because he buys so much."

"I'm sure she does. He's a good-looking guy."

"She doesn't do it because of his looks. She appreciates what he's doing and she likes to help."

Tally kept her gaze trained out the side window so her brother wouldn't notice her watery eyes.

"He was married before."

"That doesn't surprise me. Why did his wife divorce him?"

"Jesus, Tally, what's with all this negativity? Sam's wife didn't divorce him, she died." He shook his head. "I'm not saying this to be mean, but I'm starting to think the neurologist's tests missed something with you."

Her head whipped back to face him. "*What?*"

"You're a glass-half-full girl, not a Negative Nelly. I've never known you to be anything but upbeat, and I'm pretty sure you know that's the truth, otherwise you wouldn't be crying right now."

Tally swiped at her cheeks. What Micah said seemed right. She used to be a fun-loving person. So, what was wrong with her now?

"I know Mom wants to have a happy-family reunion dinner tonight, but I think I need to be by myself for a while. Will you let her know?"

"Yeah," he said, drawing out the word, "but she's not going to like it."

"I'll be okay. Two doctors gave me the A-OK, right?"

He nodded, but didn't look convinced.

"I have some thinking to do, and I need to do it alone. Let's go."

"Maybe you should tell Mom yourself."

"Tell her I *promise* to be there tomorrow night."

"Okay, but don't be surprised if she calls you…or shows up at your door."

"If I'm sleeping—"

"You know she has a key, right?"

Tally gave up. "I'll call her myself."

Micah nodded. "Good idea."

They drove in silence after that, but something else kept rolling around in her head.

Dr. Dixon had held her back and said one last thing. *If you find that you aren't the same person you were before the accident, don't let it get you down. It's entirely possible you'll find that other Tally again and she'll be more than happy to come out and play.*

At the time, she'd stared at him, speechless and nonplussed, wondering if he was a real doctor, or playing at one, uttering a medical diagnosis like that.

Funny how things turned out.

Right this minute, she understood his words exactly, and she hoped like hell he was right.

Chapter 5

Tally considered herself lucky to have found the apartment she lived in. Aside from being in a great neighborhood, it had been completely refurbished, including a dream kitchen (if only she cooked!), but for her, the icing on her little cupcake was the gas fireplace. Not only was it great for snowy days and evenings, but it created a terrific ambiance for thinking.

She made herself comfortable on the floor in front of the hearth, sipping a cup of tea, staring into the flames.

Grey Dixon had told her not to force her memories, to simply let them come. Easy for him to say, since he didn't have amnesia. How could she *not* think nonstop about the memories she'd lost?

The problem was, she'd always leaned toward impatience. She was anxious to recover those memories now, not six weeks or six months down the road. Determined to dredge up *some*thing, she focused on her job at Tidwell's.

From the back of her mind, she snagged the remnant of a conversation between her and Madelyn Haversham, Tidwell's HR director. *We're sorry we have to cut your hours, Tally. I know you aren't crazy about your duties here, but you're one of the best workers we've ever had.*

"Of course, I was," Tally muttered to the flames. "I don't do anything halfway. Ever."

On the heels of that came another conversation between her and Bonnie, when she'd stopped by Gingerbread Cottage to do some Christmas shopping.

That stopped her short. Had she actually liked Christmas last year? Was that why she'd she been Christmas shopping?

I'm sorry to hear you got your hours cut, Bonnie had said, *but if you're interested, I could certainly use another person to help me out here. What do you say?*

It shocked Tally to remember she'd said *yes* without giving it a second thought. She needed the job, if she wanted to continue to eat and pay her rent. But, there had to be other jobs she could have done. Why accept a job at a Christmas store if she hated Christmas? Surely, that would have affected her ability to make sales.

Her mother's words chose that moment to come back to her. *Sylvie was giving you pointers and Bonnie and the FruityCakes owners were impressed with your ability to merchandise and increase sales.*

Stymied, she finished her tea, pondering the ambiguity of what her mother had said. Merchandise and increase sales? Well, that certainly was different than Tidwell's, where she'd done boring data entry all day long, five days a week, ad nauseum.

Thinking of Tidwell's brought back another memory of the guy she'd run into every day at the elevator. He'd finally asked her out, but she'd discovered soon enough that he was one of those married men who got away with cheating by not wearing a wedding ring.

Micah was right. The guy was a douche bag. The bastard had broken her heart, but more than that, he'd made her distrust men until…OMG!

Sam Reed!

A little flutter teased her insides. "What the heck?" she murmured, wondering what that flutter was all about.

Unexpectedly, she remembered the day Sam had

walked into the Cottage to see Bonnie.

She'd felt that flutter then, too.

Tally found another memory. Bonnie had told her all about Sam…he was a great guy, and even though a spark or two had passed between them, they decided they'd make better friends than lovers.

Something Granny Marigold always said came on the heels of that memory. *When you don't get something you want, it's because something better is coming along.*

Bonnie had bypassed a relationship with Sam, but she'd found Griff Conte, and according to Micah, the two of them had married almost a year ago.

Tally sighed. She'd pined after Jon Avery for two years, and then one day, he'd asked her out. That relationship had gone south after three months, when she'd encountered him and his pregnant wife in the elevator, arguing about his work hours. God worked in mysterious ways to keep people informed.

How would things have worked out between her and Sam if she hadn't been hit by a drunk driver? Would they be just friends? Or would they have moved forward and become lovers? He was easy on the eyes, for sure, and he must work out, because he filled out his sweater and jeans in a hunky kind of way.

Her heart did a little flip, thinking about the two of them naked, in bed.

A subtle noise at the front door diverted her from her unanticipated carnal daydreams.

Tally rose and looked out the front window, but saw no activity outside. Curious, she peered out the peep hole in the door. No one there. Throwing caution to the wind, she opened the door, wielding her umbrella. No predator or good-looking firefighter lurked on the door mat.

Something was there, though. A small box, wrapped in pretty paper and a flourish of ribbons.

Tally hesitated. Even she knew enough to remember you couldn't trust stray packages on your front doorstep these days. Did it contain a bomb? Had someone sent anthrax for Christmas? Was it a ricin-laced fruit cake?

After a moment of staring down at the gaily wrapped box—all the while, freezing her buns off—she bent down to retrieve it. Though it was small, it had some weight to it. Ignoring the warning bells in her head, she stepped back inside and closed the door against the frigid cold.

She held the box up to her ear and drew back in surprise when she discerned a slight ticking sound. Dear God, what if it *was* a bomb? She shook it next, then realized if it was, it was entirely possible she could set it off.

After a moment's hesitation, she hurried to the kitchen and set the box on her antique pine table. She picked up her phone and moved to the doorway. Who should she call, the cops or the fire department?

Following a lengthy internal debate, she accessed her FAVORITES, intending to call her brother. Two names below Micah's, she noticed Sam Reed's number.

Hunh. Karma, or dumb luck? Only time would tell which it would be.

She tapped Sam's name and hit the speaker button as the call went through.

"Hello?" came the cautious greeting.

"Sam?"

"Yeah." A slight pause ensued. "Why are you calling, Tally?"

Of course, he knew it was her. If she had his number in her phone, he'd have her number in his, and caller ID would have let him know it was her calling. "I, um, that is, I heard something outside, and when I opened the door, I found a present on the doormat, so I brought it inside and I thought I heard it ticking."

"Ticking? You mean like a bomb ticking? Jesus, Tally. Get out of your apartment right now. I'm on my way."

He disconnected before she could defend her actions. Belatedly, she realized her actions were indefensible, but still, leave her apartment? When it was freezing outside, literally?

Instead, she put her head close to the box again. Yep,

definitely ticking. Would someone actually go to all the trouble of wrapping a bomb so beautifully? And aside from that, who'd want her dead, anyway? Maybe she *should* wait outside.

Less than five minutes passed before a heavy pounding sounded at her front door. She opened it to find not only Sam there, but Jake Rendow, a local cop who'd gone to school with her brothers.

Obviously angry, Sam said, "I told you to get out of the apartment."

"It's cold outside," she said, as if that were the only and best excuse ever. She lifted her arm and gave her hand a little wave. "Hi, Jakey."

"Hi, Tally. I'm glad to see you're out of the coma, but Sam's right. You should've left the apartment."

The two men shared a glance, then Sam said, "The bomb squad is on the way."

"Bomb squad!" she squeaked. "Christmas Valley has a bomb squad?"

"Every county has one these days," Jake said. "It's the kind of world we live in now."

Tally found that supremely depressing, even though she'd had a similar thought earlier. "Come in. You're letting all the heat out." She stepped aside so they could enter.

"Where is it?" Sam asked.

"In the kitchen, on the table." She returned his angry stare with one of her own. "Do you know where the kitchen is?"

He shook his head with disgust. "I was having coffee there with your family this morning, if you'll recall."

Tally's face grew warm. Of course, he had. Was this amnesia in retrograde, or something?

A siren sounded in the distance.

"Stay here," Jake ordered her.

Tally closed the door and reached for a sweater hanging from the coat rack.

Moments later, another fist pounded on her door. She

opened it and said, "That way," pointing toward the kitchen. Three men filed past her, sparing not a word or a glance in her direction.

She stepped outside and walked to the end of the sidewalk, praying that the men inside her apartment would live to talk about the bomb that she hoped wasn't really a bomb.

Five minutes later, the same three men came back out and trudged by her to the van they'd arrived in. There was no sign of Sam or Jake.

"You can go back inside," one of the men said as he climbed into the stepvan plainly marked BOMB SQUAD.

Shivering, Tally made her way back into her apartment. In the kitchen, she stared in shock at the old-fashioned alarm clock sitting on the counter. "It doesn't look like a bomb."

"That's because it isn't," Jake said. "It's nothing but a plain old alarm clock."

Tally frowned. Not exactly plain. "It looks like a Christmas alarm clock."

"I'd have to agree," Sam said. "According to the attached tag, it came from After Thoughts, over on Ambrose Street."

After Thoughts. That was next door to Lise's Dennison's shop, Katydid's. Lise was Mare's sister and Mare was married to Tally's brother, Derek. Lise was a whiz at designing mother–daughter coordinated clothing and other beautiful garments. Someday, Tally planned to have enough extra cash on hand to buy something beautiful to wear from Katydid's. "Can I see the card?" She held out her hand and Sam passed it over to her. Their fingertips touched and a tingle raced up her arm.

She pulled out her phone and dialed After Thoughts. "Hi, Jackie, it's Tally Barrow."

"Tally, hello! I heard you were out of the coma. I imagine your family is over the moon about you being among the living again."

"They are." So surprised that she remembered the name

of the After Thoughts owner, she almost forgot why she'd called Jackie Kincannon. "I found a package on my front porch and" —she decided not to go into details about the response that box had created— "I was wondering if you could tell me who purchased it. There doesn't seem to be a gift card with it."

"Gosh, Tally, as we get closer to Christmas, I sell and wrap so many gifts for people. Can you be a little more specific?"

Tally described the beautiful paper and ribbons, but was less excited about describing the ridiculous Christmas clock. Still, she managed it.

"Hold on, will you? I need to check something…." She came back on the line. "I know this sounds weird, but I thought that clock was still on the shelf. I'm sure I would have remembered if I'd sold it to someone."

"So you didn't wrap this box?"

"I'm pretty sure I didn't. Can you take a picture and send it to me?"

Tally accessed her camera phone, snapped the photo, and sent it.

A few moments later, Jackie said, "It's beautiful wrap, but it's not mine."

"And you didn't deliver the package to my door?"

"No."

"Well, then, who did?"

"I'm afraid I have no idea."

Tally stared at the clock. "Is it returnable?"

"I suppose so, though I can't give you a refund, since it was never sold."

"Are you saying it was shoplifted?"

"No…I mean, I don't think so. I keep a sharp eye on everyone who comes in the shop." She hesitated. "The thing is, I pulled up my inventory spreadsheet just now and it's still listed as in-stock."

"Are you open tomorrow?"

"No, I don't start staying open on Sunday until next week. I open at nine on Monday, though."

"Fine. I'll see you then." Tally wondered why she felt compelled to see the last of the Christmas alarm clock as quickly as possible.

Chapter 6

Sam much rather would have spent the evening at home, alone, thinking about Tally and where their relationship might go now that she was out of the coma.

He'd taken it as a good sign that she'd called him about the ticking present, but by the time all was said and done, he got nothing but the cold shoulder as she walked him to the door. Even her *goodbye* had icicles dripping from it.

He climbed out of his truck and made his way up to Fergus Sullivan's front door. The joke was really on him. It was obvious his budding relationship with Tally was going nowhere now. In fact, in the three short days he'd known her before the accident, it was entirely possible it hadn't been going anywhere, anyway, and he was kidding himself that it was.

With a smile plastered on his face, he knocked on the door.

Livvy O'Donnell answered.

His smile faded. Great, just what he needed, a psychic to psychic-analyze him. Fergus was one sly old coot.

"Don't go thinking I'm going to psychic-analyze you, young man," Livvy said, smiling.

He'd never had a personal encounter with Livvy over

dinner, nor had she ever climbed inside his head before. Or at least, not that he knew of. "The thought never crossed my mind," he said, lying through his teeth.

Livvy laughed. "If you say so. Come in and get warm. Fergus is fixing his famous Irish stew for dinner, along with his personal recipe for Irish soda bread. You're in for a treat."

The retired doctor had pitched in as a cook one stormy night at the firehouse while the company had been out fighting a fire. They'd come back to a huge pot of chili simmering on the gas range. If Fergus's Irish stew was anything like that chili, Livvy was right.

He slipped out of his coat and handed it over to her to hang in the guest closet. He knew from Murph, Livvy's son, that his mother and the doctor, who was the father of Murph's wife, Esme, had become fast friends. The fact that they lived next door to each other had helped cement their friendship.

"Hi, Sam," Franny Nelson called from the kitchen.

Sam responded in kind.

Livvy linked her arm though his. "You've had a rough day. How about an icy cold beer to go with your stew?"

He smiled down at her. Psychic or not, how could you not like the enchanting Olivia Strangewayes? "Sounds good."

Franny finished placing the silverware on the table, then went to give him a hug. "So good to see you, Sam."

"You, too, Franny." Frances Nelson was the mother of Charley and Stevie, who owned FruityCakes. She and Fergus were now what his mother would've called *an item*. "Hi, Fergus."

Fergus waved his wooden spoon in the air, then gave the stew pot a stir. "Glad you could join us, Sam."

Like he'd really had a choice. "Me, too."

The conversation centered around the weather for a while, then, as they took their seats at the table, Livvy mentioned the woman Sam had fallen for the moment he'd set eyes on her. "Tally's a lucky girl."

"She certainly is," Franny concurred, "and my girls and Bonnie are excited about having her back at the Cottage."

Fergus passed the soda bread basket. "Heard from Grey that she passed neurology muster with flying colors."

"I saw her when she came in," Sam said. "Grey and I were having coffee."

"How did she look to you?" Franny asked. She buttered her bread, then passed the butter to Sam.

"She *looks* like the old Tally."

"Oh, dear," Livvy said, as if her psychic ability had deduce the unspoken *but* at the end of his sentence.

Sam focused on buttering his own wedge of bread and said it, anyway. "But, she doesn't act like the old Tally."

Livvy leaned over and covered his big hand with hers and gave it a squeeze. "Don't you worry about that, Sam. Tally has some demons to battle, but once she's won that war, she'll be her old self again." She reclaimed her hand and picked up her spoon.

Sam put down his knife, frowning. "How can you be so sure?"

"I don't know how I know these things, but I do." Livvy shrugged. "You'll have to take my word for it."

That was about as clear as mud, but Sam took hope, nonetheless. Word around town was, Livvy never made a mistake when it came to matters of the heart.

Conversation after that ran to who was pregnant and when their babies were due.

Bonnie Conte was expecting her little bundle of joy any day. It was obvious Griff was crazy-in-love with her by the way he pampered her.

Joss Kringle was pregnant, but her baby wasn't due until May. Her husband, Lachlan, told anyone who would listen how excited he was about fatherhood. His parents, Kris and Nick, who owned the Christmas Valley Inn, were ecstatic over having their son back, not to mention gaining a daughter and grandbabies.

Stevie Pope was pregnant with triplets and her sister, Charley Brewster, had birthed a set of triplets in August.

"They both carried the hyperovulation gene," Fergus explained, "which passed down to them from their father." Their respective husbands, Spenser and Tate, had bets going about the combined birth weights of the next set of triplets. Whoever came closest would claim a huge pot of cash, which currently sat at five hundred and ten dollars. Word had it, the sheriff had placed his guess months ago, guaranteeing that no one would be charged with illegal gambling.

Rory Dawson had presented her husband, Coop, with a beautiful daughter the previous spring. Livvy's daughter-in-law, Esme, had a due date of January 15. Murph was thinking of either adding on to their house, or building a new one, since their family was growing. "I suggested to them that we trade houses," Livvy said. "I don't like climbing steps anymore, and my house has double the square footage."

"Did they take you up on it?" Fergus asked.

"They're thinking about it. For one thing, Arran would have some privacy, and since he's not that far away from being a teenager, I'm sure he'd like that."

"Seems like a sensible idea," Franny said. "Mom and I are trying to talk Stevie and Spense into letting us move out to the cottage. It's plenty big enough for the two of us and it would give them some privacy."

"Why do you have to ask permission?" Livvy asked.

"We're not. They're worried they'd be kicking us out, but what do Granny and I need with a big ole house like that?"

Fergus looked as if he really wanted to contribute to the conversation, but held his tongue. Instead, he directed the conversation back to who was expecting. Sean and Lily D'Arcy had said they were done contributing to the world population at four kids, but Lily, too, was expecting in March, as was Sylvie Barrow, Tally's sister-in-law.

Sam was happy for all his friends, but he craved having children of his own. When his wife had died a few years earlier of cancer, his dream of being a father had died too.

Truth be told, his relationship with Missy had died a horrible death long before then, when she'd moved into the second bedroom and refused to have sex with him. She'd decided she didn't want to be a mother after all, and wouldn't risk even the slightest chance she might get pregnant.

As life's ironies sometimes happened, before Sam could decide how to handle that glitch in his marriage, Missy was diagnosed with ovarian cancer. She was already at stage four by then, and she refused all possible treatments. Sam wanted to take care of her at home, but Missy had checked herself into hospice care and died three days later.

He'd taken that hard. He'd exchanged vows with her that said *in sickness and in health*, and he wasn't the kind of man who shirked a promise.

And now, years later life threw him another curve ball. He hadn't expected to be wowed by Tally Barrow, then lose her. He'd prayed for her recovery every day, but though he'd hoped his prayers would be answered, deep down, he'd never believed they would be.

"Sam?"

Pulled from his musing, he started. "Sorry, my mind wandered."

"Would you care for more stew?" Livvy asked, giving him a knowing smile.

He resisted squirming in his chair. "Actually, I would. It really hits the spot tonight." Hoping to divert his brain from thoughts of Tally, he moved on to another topic. "I heard you're hanging up your doctor shingle, Fergus."

His host glanced at Franny, then back at him. "Not an actual practice," he said. "The hospital has asked me to come on as an on-call orthopedic specialist, since they've been unable to attract anyone in that field as yet."

Sam frowned. "I thought they had someone lined up."

"They did, but he backed out at the last minute. His wife prefers to live in a large city, and that's definitely not what we are here."

"Thank goodness," Livvy said.

Franny nodded her agreement.

"Are you inclined to accept?" Sam asked.

"Possibly. I'm no spring chicken, you know, but I believe I can handle the number of orthopedic emergencies they see here in a year."

He shared another look with Franny.

"I know you're dying to tell them," she said. "Go ahead."

He smiled at her.

"Oh, for heaven's sake, Fergus," Livvy said with an exaggerated sigh.

The retired doctor shook his head at her. "You already know, don't you?"

"Of course, but Sam doesn't."

Being a smart guy, Sam said, "I'm guessing you and Franny are finally going to tie the knot?"

Franny giggled.

Fergus grinned. "We certainly are."

"Congratulations!"

"Thank you," the happy couple replied in unison.

"Have you set a date?" Sam asked.

Fergus and Franny glanced at Livvy, who said, "What? Just because I knew you were getting married doesn't mean I know what date you picked out."

"Valentine's Day," Franny said.

Fergus nodded. "We thought we best avoid the rush at the Christmas Valley Inn for all the young lovers' weddings."

Three sets of eyes pinned Sam in place, with a spoon halfway to his mouth. "Why are you looking at me?"

Livvy tittered.

"No reason," Franny said.

Fergus concentrated on his soda bread instead of responding.

Sam glanced at Livvy. "What do you know that I don't know?"

"Not a thing," she said, wiping her mouth with her napkin. "Except that everything works out in the end."

Sam stuffed his spoon into his mouth, wondering if he should ask for further clarification. He decided not to. He didn't want to make a bigger fool of his lovesick self than he already was.

Tally snuggled under a blanket in front of the fire, almost wishing she hadn't talked her mother into having a family dinner on Sunday instead of tonight.

She, who never lacked for something to do, or someone to do it with, was lonely.

She thought about Micah's dog and wondered if she should get one of her own. With a startled jerk, she remembered she already had a dog. Buttercup was a golden retriever, like Micah's. She reached for her phone and dialed her brother. "Where's my dog?"

"I wondered how long it would take you to remember you had one," he said. "She's here and I'll bring her by any time you want."

Was she ready to take care of a dog, when she hadn't even remembered she *had* a dog? "Give me a few more days to acclimate."

"Sounds good, and don't worry. She's been well taken care of here. Gotta go. 'Bye."

Of course he had to go. He had a lovely wife to spend this cold, snowy evening with, didn't he?

Sans a man, she carried on thinking about one. Sam, to be exact.

What was he doing tonight?

Who was he doing it with?

Was whoever he was doing something with a woman?

The little green jealousy monster reared its ugly head inside her, which surprised the heck out of Tally. How could she possibly be possessive over someone she couldn't even remember, or barely remembered, as the case may be?

She thought about calling him, just to hear his voice. She could apologize for ushering him out of her apartment earlier without so much as a *thank you*.

In retrospect, she couldn't believe how rude she'd been, so she really *did* owe him an apology. She hadn't thanked Jake, either, and she'd known him since she was kid. She might have a lot of faults, but rudeness had never been one of them. Her brother was right. She wasn't herself.

She reached for her phone, but before she could plug in her password, the stupid Christmas clock alarm sounded.

The only reason she recognized it was because it had gone off earlier, while she was eating her solitary dinner. Hearing "Jingle Bell Rock" break the silence had made her jump about a foot.

Why was it going off again, when she'd shut off the alarm function? And beyond that, how did a wind-up alarm clock even have the capability to play a Christmas tune?

Irritated, because she was comfortable in front of the fire, she got to her feet, let the blanket drop to the floor, and traipsed into the kitchen, where the clock sat on the countertop. As before, the hands indicated midnight straight up. Out of perversity, Tally had wound the clock and set it to the proper time. There was no way in heck the clock could have advanced six hours, when only two had passed.

She picked up the blasted thing and shook it, like that would make it shut up. When it didn't, she turned it over and pushed in the pin to silence it.

Quiet, finally.

She reset the time, then shook her finger at the clock. "No more tricks, understand?"

Tick, tick, tick, tick.

"That's better."

But the question remained, how had the darned thing reset itself, and why?

Chapter 7

Tally prowled her apartment in darkness. There was something about street lights and snow that seemed to make the outside brighter, which helped her get around without stubbing a toe, plus, she'd left all the window coverings open, which also helped.

Ordinarily, she would have closed the blinds for heat conservation, but these weren't ordinary circumstances. For one thing, she was barely out of a coma that had lasted nearly twelve months. For another, she wasn't sleepy, and she didn't even feel tired, so why go to bed?

After missing almost a year of living, there wasn't much else she could do in the middle of the night. She might as well go window-to-window and enjoy looking out at her snowy surroundings.

All traces of medical equipment had been cleared away by her parents, and for that she was grateful. She felt restless, but what could she do about it? It was two a.m. Everyone she knew would be in bed, asleep, or maybe doing something else if they had a nice, warm body snuggled up next to them.

That brought her to a stop as her mind shot off on a new tangent. Snuggling up next to Sam Reed. Just the thought of it made her heart race a little faster.

She shook her head, trying to clear the vision from her mind.

What was wrong with her? Was she so horny she'd latch on to the only single guy she could think of?

Possibly. She'd never gone to bed with Jon Avery, thank goodness, and before that, her first and last serious relationship had ended five years earlier. So, yes, maybe she *was* horny.

She ventured into the living room and turned on the TV to the Hallmark Channel. Being November, a Christmas-themed love story was playing. Tally sank down onto the sofa to watch.

Immediately, she became engaged in the story of a woman fighting off her attraction to a man trying to purchase her parents' inn. An overused trope, but at least it wasn't the worn-out old-boyfriend-from-high-school plot.

At four, another movie came on. Tally watched that, too. This time it was about a woman whose husband had died. She had no interest in finding someone to replace him three years later, but the male lead had other ideas.

That made Tally sit back and think. Sam's wife had died and he'd lived for several years without even dating, if what Bonnie had told her was correct. What had changed for him? Did men have ticking biological clocks? Was he in the market for kids and she was a convenient single woman he could hook up with? Or, was it possible…had he *felt* something for her?

The possibility that he actually cared about her left her confused, and if she were being honest with herself, feeling a little warm and gooey inside. Despite her intention not to, she embraced the sensation and continued to watch the movie.

A few minutes later, the Christmas alarm clock blared "Jingle Bell Rock," startling her.

Irritated, Tally hit the PAUSE button on the remote and tore off for the kitchen. She stared at the clock, perplexed.

Both hands pointed straight up at the twelve.

Why?

How?

What did it mean?

This time, after she shut it off and reset the time, she wrapped masking tape around the clock to hold the alarm button in. After that, she stuffed it into her dish towel drawer.

She swiped her hands together. "That oughta do it."

She went back to watching the movie and promptly fell asleep on the sofa.

Several hours later, she awoke to the alarm clock sounding off. Again.

Disoriented, she jerked to a sitting position, then bolted to her feet.

How on earth could the alarm sound so loud from a drawer, and why did it keep ringing?

When she reached the kitchen, she discovered that not only was the Christmas clock *not* in the drawer, but the masking tape she'd wrapped around it was nowhere to be seen. Again, the two hands indicated the time to be midnight, or noon, depending on your perspective.

She smacked the side of her head, as if that would dispel what remained of her drowsiness. "Think!" Minutes later, the plan she came up with seemed not only foolish, but ridiculous. She didn't care, because it might work.

Tally headed to the storage closet conveniently nestled at the end of the short hallway that led to her bedroom. There, she pulled out a roll of duct tape and took it back to the kitchen, where she opened the cupboard holding her storage containers. She quickly located a size that would hold the clock.

Next, she yanked open her neatly arranged junk drawer and grabbed the scissors. She wrapped the duct tape tightly around the clock three times, then set it inside the container, which she wrapped both vertically and horizontally with duct tape, again three times.

Once that was done, she went to her closet for an empty shoe box.

No darned Christmas clock playing "Jingle Bell Rock" was going to get the best of her!

Tally was at her wit's end.

Putting the duct-taped clock in a duct-taped container in a duct-taped shoe box hadn't worked.

Repeating the procedure, and locking the duct-taped shoe box in her grandmother's old steamer trunk, hadn't worked, either.

What next?

She stared at the Christmas clock, finally understanding what the word *flummoxed* meant. Bemused. Bothered. Bewildered. Baffled. Bring on the synonyms.

Twelve o'clock straight up and the tune it played, "Jingle Bell Rock," showed no sign of wearing down.

It hit her then where she might put the outlandish reappearing clock that it might actually stay put.

She pushed in the pin on the back, silencing the music. "Thank goodness," she muttered as she reached for the duct tape. This time, she skipped setting it to the correct time, which was obviously a wasted effort.

By the time she finished wrapping the clock, not one speck of it was visible. For all intents and purposes, she held nothing but a big lump of ticking duct tape in her hands.

She placed it in the shoe box again, and duct-taped that, as well. So far, she should've gone through more than half the roll, but each time the clock reappeared, and she grabbed the duct tape again, it was almost the full roll she'd started with. It brought to mind the sherry bottle in *The Bishop's Wife*. Cary Grant, playing the angel named Dudley, had fiddled with it so that it never emptied, no matter how much was poured from the bottle. Was an angel controlling her duct tape?

It didn't dawn on her until she traipsed out to her parking spot that her idea to lock the clock in the trunk of her

VW Beetle wasn't going to work. She'd completely spaced that she no longer had a car. Hers had been totaled when Jim Fridley hit her.

With that idea tanking, she considered an alternative location to stash the clock so that it would have no hope of escape and would *not* reappear in her kitchen. She walked toward the fenced enclosure hiding the trash toters, but at the last minute, discarded that possibility. The clock had to be returned to After Thoughts in pristine condition, not smelling like garbage. It never occurred to her to question the incongruity of her reasoning.

Clutching the box to her chest, she shivered and realized she'd come outside without a coat on. She turned and walked back toward her apartment.

A truck pulled into the lot, easing into what would have been her parking space. Tally thought about giving the driver what-for. Just because she was carless at the moment didn't mean someone else could have her assigned parking space.

"Tally, what are you doing outside with no coat on?"

She recognized the voice without turning to look. Sam What's-his-name. Why now, of all times, did he have to make an appearance? "I wasn't planning on being out but a minute," she said, hurrying toward her front door, which was standing wide open.

She came to a halt. Had she really left it that way? Worried for a moment that Grey Dixon didn't actually know a brain from a hammer toe, and she might oughta be confined to the Cuckoo's Nest, she got a little teary-eyed.

"You're shivering," Sam said, urging her across the threshold. He closed the door behind them and pulled off his coat, placing it over her shoulders.

The warmth from his big body lingered in the fabric, driving away her shivers. She looked up at him, uncertain. A single tear rolled down her cheek. "What are you doing here?"

His eyes tracked the trail of that tear, but his lips tightened at her tone. "Your mom asked me to stop and pick you up for dinner, since you don't have a car."

"My mom."

He nodded.

"You don't mind if I call her and confirm that."

"Feel free."

He glanced away, obviously hurt, but why? For all she knew, he planned to kidnap her, not take her to the folks' place for dinner.

A moment later, he pulled out his phone, called up a number, and held the phone up to her ear, since her arms were constrained beneath his coat, clutching the stupid shoebox.

"Hi, Sam," her mother's voice said.

"It's not Sam, Mom, it's me," Tally said.

"Hi, sweetie. I take it Sam's there to pick you up?"

"I wanted to confirm that he's giving me a lift to your house."

A brief pause later, her mother replied. "Is there a problem?"

"No," Tally assured her. She stared up at the firefighter. "Soon as I get my coat on, we'll be on our way."

"See you in a few, then" Jean said. "You sure everything's okay?"

How did she answer that? Tally wondered. *No, I've got this Christmas clock and it's haunted or something.* Or, *No, this hunky firefighter is lighting up my insides and I have no idea why.* Either response would be the wrong one.

"Tally?"

"Everything's fine, Mom. See you in a bit. 'Bye."

Sam's thumb hit the red dot on the screen, disconnecting the call.

His eyes met hers and she shivered again.

"What's going on?" he asked.

"You tell me."

He slid his phone back into his pocket and raised his hand to cup her face. His thumbed swiped gently at the moisture left by the tear. "I'm glad you're back with us."

She blinked in response, not sure what to say. He sounded so...proprietary. Surprisingly, it didn't bother her, and that gave her pause.

"Are you warm enough?"

She nodded.

His gaze dropped to her lips.

Tally was absolutely positive he intended to kiss her. "Sam?" she whispered.

He gave his head a little shake, as if to rouse himself from a stupor. His gaze met hers again. "What?"

"Mom said dinner's at six. It's almost that now. We should go."

His sigh was nearly inaudible. "You're right." He removed his coat with a gentleness that belied his size and pulled it back on. "What's in the box?"

Tally had no intention of telling him what had been going on with the Christmas clock since he and Jake had confirmed it wasn't a bomb. "Uh, stuff."

He frowned, but didn't pursue it, though he had to be wondering why it was so thoroughly duct-taped. "I'll get your coat. Where is it?"

She gestured toward the hall tree near the front door. There was no time now to deal with the clock. With any luck, it would still be inside the box when she returned home.

But if it wasn't....

A little green-and-red light bulb went off over her head, presenting a possible solution.

Her dad had a sledge hammer.

Darn, if only she didn't have to return the clock to After Thoughts in pristine condition!

Chapter 8

Tally scooted as close to the passenger door as she could get. Yeah, right. Like that would distance her from the sexy man driving the truck!

Who was she kidding?

Sam spoke not a word as they made their way to Tally's parents' home, which was fine with Tally. Personally, she had a lot to say, but her thoughts were so jumbled, it would be better to get them sorted out before she started babbling, like she usually did.

Her father had been busy, she noticed as they neared the Barrow homestead. All the exterior lights and yard décor were up and lit. That meant the interior would be decorated, too. Her parents had engaged in a years-long, friendly competition to see who finished decorating first, the inside queen or the outside king.

The thought of so much Christmas almost made Tally ask Sam to turn the truck around and take her home.

In turn, that made her think of all the Christmas boxes in her closet. Before the crash, she knew she must've liked the holiday. Otherwise, why would she have boxes and boxes of Christmas décor, or hired Sylvie to decorate Micah's house, and why would she have agreed to work at the Gingerbread Cottage?

Sam pulled up at the curb on the opposite side of the street. "Looks like everyone's here."

Tally scanned the cars. By *everyone*, she knew he meant family, which begged the question, why had he been included, when he wasn't related to a single one of them? "Looks like."

"Stay put until I get around to open your door. Mr. Salisbury hasn't cleared his walk yet."

"Okay." She thought it was nice, the way Sam showed her parents' elderly neighbor some respect with the Mr. title, but how did he know Emil Salisbury?

Several moments later, Sam opened her door and offered her a hand.

Tally undid her seat belt and slid her hand into his after a brief hesitation. Once her feet were on the ground, she looked up at the man who had the power to excite her without even trying. He was studying the snowy sidewalk.

He glanced at her with a smile. "I should be able to get it done before dinner." And with that, he closed the truck door and led her across the street, keeping a firm hold on her arm. He rang the doorbell and a few seconds later, Bryan opened the door.

After greetings, Sam asked, "Have you spoken to Emil today?"

Bryan nodded. "His arthritis is acting up. I told him I'd get the walk tomorrow."

"I'll do it now," Sam said.

Her father gave him an affectionate pat on the shoulder. "You know where the snow shovel is."

Sam grinned. "I do. Be back shortly." He gave Tally a look that sizzled her insides, then pulled the door closed.

"He's really going to shovel Emil's walk now?" Tally asked.

"He's really going over to shovel *all* Emil's concrete surfaces."

"Oh."

"Let me take your coat, honey. Everyone's in the kitchen, and anxious to see you."

Tally unbuttoned her coat and slipped it off. "Does Sam do that often?"

Her father looked down at her. "Well, yeah. That's the kind of man he is. Last winter, when we spent so much time at the hospital and at your place, he came every time it snowed and shoveled our sidewalk, the driveway, and the walkway. Sean enlisted his help with the snowplow, too, so our street and all the streets leading from here to the hospital and your place were plowed, too."

"As a firefighter, doesn't he have to be at work?"

"He has one day on and two days off. If it snowed while he was working, he got one of his buddies to help out."

"He sounds too good to be true," she said, her tone a little snarkier than she'd intended.

Her father shot her a quizzical glance. "He has a good heart, Tally."

Is that why Sam Reed made her insides tingle, because he had a good heart? She wasn't buying it, not after the way Jon Avery, the douche bag, had fooled her.

Bryan hung her coat in the guest closet, then took her hand and tugged her toward the kitchen, where everyone seemed to be in good spirits. Of the five Barrow siblings, only the two brothers, Micah and Derek, were married.

Tally hung back in the doorway, studying her family. She, Tessa, and Jennie must be the losers, because they were still single. Derek, the oldest, was married to Sean D'Arcy's sister, Mare, and of course, Micah was married to Sylvie. The moment she saw Sylvie, the memory of hiring her to decorate her brother's house came flooding back. Micah, a Marine, had been injured in action, and ready to leave the service after ten years. His and Sylvie's story was something of a fairy-tale romance, the kind Tally had always longed for.

Was that why she'd fallen for Jon Avery? He'd seemed like Prince Charming? Looking back, the creep didn't hold a candle to Sam.

All the grandkids were situated in the family room

watching *Rudolph, the Red-Nosed Reindeer*.

The moment the adults noticed her, Tally was inundated with hugs. Everyone had so many questions, but Tally had no answers. How was she supposed to remember what it felt like to be in a coma? At the moment, she still couldn't remember the crash that had put her there.

Chatter continued through dinner, and afterward, her nieces and nephews begged her to play UNO with them. Tally begged off, quite frankly, exhausted from all the commotion. By eight o'clock, she was ready to slink off to her own place, where she could crawl into bed and escape the world.

"You ready to go?" Sam asked.

Tally turned her head in his direction, surprised. "How'd you know?"

He grinned. "ESP."

She almost grinned back. "As if. Do you think they'd mind?"

"No. In fact, I'm pretty sure they're expecting you to cut out early."

Tally glanced at her mother, who gave her a slight nod. She took a deep breath and announced to the family, "Much as I'd like to stay, and as incongruous as it sounds, I'm really tired. Time for me to head home."

Hugs, goodbyes, tears, and more hugs lasted a good twenty minutes, until, finally, she and Sam were able to step out the door.

Tally had never been so glad to escape a family event, even if the getaway was with a man she really didn't know, and didn't quite trust.

Sam kept shooting her concerned glances as he drove and finally asked, "You doing okay?"

"I'm a little overwhelmed."

"I can only imagine."

At her place, he once again took her parking space and

hurried around to open her door. "I'll walk you to up."

"Thank you."

Once at the landing, he shoved his hands into his pockets. "I know you were going to take the clock back to After Thoughts tomorrow, but if you can wait a day, I'll give you a lift." When she turned a questioning glance on him, he explained. "I'm on tomorrow and you don't have transportation."

Ah, yes. One day on, two days off, and he was right. She had no car. Would it really hurt to hold off for a day to take the clock back? "It's nice of you to offer. Thanks."

They stood staring at each other without speaking.

Tally didn't notice the cold.

Apparently, neither did Sam.

Finally, he said, "You should go inside. It's freezing out here."

She wasn't quite sure why, but she asked, "Would you like to come in for a hot chocolate?"

Sam practically did a double-take. "Sure."

Tally dug into her pocket for her key and unlocked the door. She stepped inside, overwhelmingly aware of the man behind her. She tossed her key on the side table and pulled off her gloves, stuffing them into her pockets.

Sam closed and locked the door behind them, then helped her remove her coat. He hung it on the same hook he'd taken it from earlier. His went up next to it.

Hot chocolate. Tally had to get to the kitchen to make it, but all she could do was stare up at Sam, like some idiot school girl crushing on a guy she couldn't have.

"What's wrong?" he asked.

"I don't know what's going on here."

Sam's jaw worked furiously, as if he had something to say, but couldn't bring himself to utter the words.

Tally went on. "I don't actually remember you from before, but being around you…thinking about you…it makes me feel funny inside."

He frowned. After a moment's hesitation, he asked, "Funny, like how?"

"Tingly."

His eyes flared.

"Excited."

He glanced away briefly.

"Anxious."

His smoldering gaze came back to meet hers.

"What does it all mean, Sam?"

"Before I say, can I tell you something?"

"Yes."

"I feel all those things, too."

"You do?"

"I do."

"But what does it mean?" she persisted.

"We're attracted to each other."

"We are?"

He nodded. "I've only felt something like this one other time."

"With you wife?"

Again, he nodded. "It wasn't this intense, though."

"I'm so confused."

"I'm not."

She tilted her head at him. "Why not?"

"Because."

"That's no answer."

"Actually, it's an answer with a wealth of meaning behind it."

She shook her head. "You're going to have to be a little clearer than that."

"Can I show you instead?"

Tally didn't see how that would be possible, but she said, "Yes."

Before she could prepare, he lowered his head and kissed her.

Without thinking, Tally pressed against him, sliding her arms around his neck. It had to be right, because her body said it was exactly where it was supposed to be, doing exactly what it should be doing. And by body, she meant *her*.

If someone had asked how long that kiss lasted, she wouldn't have been able to say. In fact, she probably wouldn't have been able to answer, period. All the emotions she'd admitted to him blossomed into fireworks with other emotions she couldn't even define. The resulting explosion was like nothing she'd ever experienced before. As far as she was concerned, the kiss could go on forever. It was that amazing.

When he finally released her lips, Sam barely moved, resting his forehead against hers. "We have chemistry, Tally."

"Chemistry?" she asked, dazed.

"Sparks?" he prompted.

She couldn't disagree. "Should we do something about it?" It was a daring question, and she probably shouldn't have asked it, but she wasn't sorry she had. She could hardly wait to hear his answer.

"We could."

His tone carried no doubt, but she nonetheless discerned a small reservation behind those two words. "How long did I know you before the car crash?"

"Three days."

"Did we do anything about these sparks then?"

"We came close."

"How close?"

He nestled closer to her body, if that was even possible. "Close."

His erection pressed against her belly, throwing her into some kind of carnal frenzy, the likes of which she'd never faced until that moment. "Sam?"

"Hmm?" His lips sought her ear and his tongue toyed gently with the lobe.

Tally shivered. "If we were to do something about it, would it mean we'd take our clothes off?"

His voice caught. "If that's what you want."

"I don't *know* if that's what I want," she whispered, "but it feels like that's what I need, and I need it badly." She turned her head, seeking his mouth again. She opened her lips to invite his tongue in for a lover's duel. She didn't pull away until quite some time later. "Do we know each other well enough to have sex?"

"It would be more than sex, Tally."

"What more is there than sex?"

"Making love."

"Making love." Tally rolled that around in her mind. She liked the idea of it and what it implied.

"We never got that far before," he admitted, "but I'm pretty sure we both knew that the sex between us would be out of this world."

"Really?" she asked, but wondered why, since she was certain he was right.

He blinked at her, then took her mouth again. As responses went, it was totally informative.

Tally accepted his answer, but had to ask, "We really liked each other enough before the crash to make love?"

"Yes."

"Will you think less of me if I take off all my clothes and drag you into my bed after I've only known you for four days?"

Something that sounded like a strangled laugh came from deep in his throat.

"Are you laughing at me?"

"Never." He went in for another earth-shattering kiss. When he came up for air, he said, "You may have only known me for four days total, Tally, but I've know you for almost a year."

She moved back enough to study his expression...to examine the secrets in his dark chocolate eyes. Disappointed by what she thought she saw, she asked, "So, that's a no-go for getting naked together?"

"I would never think less of you for anything." He shook his head. "See, we're doing so much catch-up, when there's explaining to do, and questions to answer."

"I'm learning as I go."

"I know you are," he said in a gentle voice, so at odds with his size.

Knowing that she might be tempting fate, and his patience, she did have more of those questions he referred to, and she absolutely had to have the answers. "How long were you and your wife married?"

"Seven years."

"How many women have you dated since she died?"

"Two. You and Bonnie, although Bonnie and I recognized right away that we'd make better friends than lovers."

"Does that mean that you and I recognized right away we'd make better lovers than friends?"

"Not exactly," he said. "We recognized that we'd be great friends, and exceptional lovers."

"I can't believe we actually discussed it."

"We didn't," he admitted, "but as I said before, I'm certain we both knew that sex between us would be mind-blowing."

"You've convinced me." If there was one thing Tally knew about herself, it was that she was a risk-taker. "Enough talk. Let's have some action."

Before she knew what was happening, Sam had her in his arms, carrying her down the short hallway to her bedroom.

Tally had never envisioned how the perfect seduction would go, but as far as she was concerned, this was it.

She only hoped Sam wouldn't regret it later.

Chapter 9

Sam had Tally's clothes off so fast, she didn't fully comprehend until she stood naked in front of him what they were *really* about to do.

She needed Sam in the worst way. She needed to feel his body, to stroke every inch of him, to taste him, to welcome him into her body. "Hurry, Sam," she pleaded, working at the buckle of his belt.

"I am," he said, unable to take his eyes off her. "Pull back the covers."

Tally nodded. In less time than it took to say, *Let's have sex ten times tonight*, the bedding was flipped back. She turned to Sam, overcome by the beauty of his well-honed flesh. Muscular, but not on WWF overload. She laid a hand on his chest, over his heart. "Your pulse is running rampant."

"Because of you," he said. In the next instant, he grabbed her and they both went down on the bed.

They kissed, they tasted, they touched, they explored. When she begged him to take her, he did. He was gentle and intense and fierce all at once. Though she knew the odds were against it, they climaxed together, then lay in a sweaty heap, him on top of her, kissing her everywhere he could reach, like he could never get enough of her.

"Sam?"

"What, sweetheart?"

"I have no words."

"Me, either."

"Did you know I don't like Christmas?"

Lavishing his attention on her breasts, his head came up. "Not true. You love Christmas."

"No, I don't. I hate it."

He raised himself up on both elbows. "Why would you even think that?"

She stared at him with troubled eyes. "I don't know. It's just that when I woke up from the coma, I knew I didn't like Christmas."

"I saw you at work in Gingerbread Cottage, Tally. You loved what you were doing there."

She shook her head. "I'm sure I didn't."

"Everyone you worked with would beg to differ with you, plus, you came to the firehouse and helped us decorate our tree and the station. You had a blast doing it, too."

Shocked, she could only stare at him, speechless. "I did not."

"Yes, you did. I have photos to prove it."

Photos? That threw her. "So, why do I think I hate Christmas, then?"

"Beats me." He went back to suckling her nipple.

"I thought I didn't like you, either."

His head came up again. He had a frown firmly in place, though his tone was wry when he said, "I kinda figured that."

"I think I may have hurt your feelings, too."

"You did, but I understood."

"I'm sorry."

"It's okay. Grey warned me that you might not remember me."

"He did?"

"Yep."

"I wish he'd warned me that I might have all these tingly feelings about you."

"He's your doctor, not your sex therapist."

"I realize that, but still, it would have been nice to have some warning that we'd end up like this."

He pushed himself off of her and sat on the edge of the bed. "Are you saying you only made love with me because you wanted to see if you actually liked me?"

She reached out and ran her hand from his shoulder down to his luscious buttock. "No, I made love with you because I couldn't help myself."

Sam leaned forward and put his elbows on his knees. He clasped his hands, prayer fashion, and dropped his head.

"What's the matter?"

"Something's wrong with this picture."

"Not with this picture," she corrected softly, then sighed. "With me."

He didn't deny it. A moment later, he stood and began pulling on his clothes.

"Are you angry?"

"No, but now I'm confused."

"Imagine how I feel."

That brought his head around to look at her. "I've been trying to do that for almost a year."

"You must've had hope, otherwise you wouldn't be right here, right now."

His wide shoulders slumped. "I'm a glass-half-full guy, Tally. I always have hope."

"Micah reminded me yesterday that I used to be a glass-half-full girl. I'm sorry I've disappointed you."

His gazed skimmed her naked body. "You haven't disappointed me, not at all, but I have some thinking to do."

Tally sighed and rolled onto her side, facing away from him, trying not to cry. "I can get another ride to After Thoughts on Tuesday."

"No, don't. I offered, I'll take you. I was thinking, after that, maybe you'd like to start looking for a replacement vehicle."

"I suppose I should."

His hand came down on her shoulder, forcing her to her back again. "Don't be upset."

"I'm not. I have some thinking to do, too."

His hand wandered down to her breasts. "You have beautiful boobs, Tally."

"Lot of good they do me," she said bitterly, surprised when he knelt over her and lowered his head so he could take a nipple into his mouth. "What are you doing?"

"Damned if I know," he said. He popped back up and shucked his trousers and boxer shorts. "What I do know is, it's early, and I haven't had near enough of you yet. I can think later."

Tally awoke to Sam's mouth on hers and his hand between her legs. She moaned over his finger imitating what his tongue was doing to hers, and then the orgasm hit, and she screamed. It went on forever and when it was done, it left her replete and virtually wasted. Every nerve in her body had been pleasured by the man she loved.

"I need to go, love. I have to be at the station at eight sharp."

"But, I should do for you what you just did for me," she protested, reaching for him. She curled her fingers around his shaft.

"Tomorrow," he said, grimacing, though not from pain.

"How long does it take you to get to the station?" she asked, edging closer to his groin.

"I have to shower."

"We can shower together, after I…."

Sam groaned, glanced at the clock, and apparently decided to let her have her way with him.

Five minutes later, they shared a shower, another orgasm, and then he was on his way.

"Pick you up in the morning for breakfast," he said. "Around nine?"

Tally could hardly wait. "Come earlier. We can eat in bed."

He wiggled his eyebrows at her suggestion. "I had no idea the prospect of breakfast in bed could be such a turn on."

She shot him a cheeky grin. "And I had no idea I'd fall for a man who likes breakfast in bed."

"Will you marry me, Tally?"

Thinking he was joking, she said, "Absolutely. Name the date."

Sam took time for one last, lingering kiss, then hurried to the front door.

Tally followed, naked, at a slower pace, locking the door behind him. She returned to her bathroom and studied her reflection in the full-length mirror on the back of the door.

Had she changed?

Did she have a scarlet L on her forehead for *loose woman*?

Did Sam really care about her?

And, an afterthought that should have been a main concern, because neither of them had come prepared for a night of marathon sex…what if she and Sam had made a baby during their hours of lovemaking?

Her hand went to her belly. With splayed fingers, she rubbed her thumb just below her navel.

Would it be so bad if they had? Sam had asked her to marry him, but she was certain he hadn't been serious. If she turned up pregnant, he'd have to ask again, and mean it.

The phone rang before she could dissect her feelings about what had happened between the two of them.

"Hello?"

"I love you," Sam said. "I just realized, I forgot to say that."

Stymied, Tally didn't respond.

"Are you there?"

"Yes. I think I love you, too."

"When will you know for sure?"

"I don't know. Maybe by the time we have breakfast in bed tomorrow morning?"

Sam laughed.

"What would you like?"

"You name it, and I'm good with it," he said, "but if all I have to feast on is you, I'll still be the happiest man on earth."

"Call me for phone sex anytime," Tally said, her tone more like a purr. "We can have appetizers whenever you like."

"Tally!"

"Are you scandalized?"

"I'm not sure."

"I am. I don't know where that came from. Do you think I have a brain injury?"

He laughed. "You did have a brain injury, remember? But Grey said you're in good shape now."

"I really need to do some heavy-duty thinking today. I need to know if I was like this before, or if my brain has been altered to make me a sex fiend." She hung up before he could respond, and when her phone rang again immediately, she declined his call.

Tally went back to the bathroom and examined her reflection once more. She ran her hands over her breasts and down her belly to the place between her legs. It would take little to achieve another orgasm, but she'd rather let Sam take care of that for her.

She brushed her teeth, then stepped back into the shower, running the water to almost cold.

She had to do something to cool her jets over the firefighter known as Sam Reed.

Chapter 10

Tally didn't bother to get dressed after her second shower. Instead, she snuggled under the covers, embracing the masculine scent Sam had left behind on her sheets. She slept another two hours, dreaming about making love with the man she thought she loved.

Around nine-thirty, she pulled on pajamas and a pair of fuzzy slippers. She made the bed, then padded around her apartment, trying to decide what to do next.

Belatedly, she remembered to let Jackie know that she wouldn't be at After Thoughts until the next day, due to lack of transportation. Tally no sooner hung up than her phone rang. It was Bonnie, from Gingerbread Cottage.

"I wanted to call sooner, but Griff advised me to let you get accustomed to being you again. How're you doing?"

"I think I'm okay. I've had medical clearances, so...."

Obviously taking that as a sign to continue, Bonnie asked, "Would you like to come back to work at the Cottage? We could really use your upbeat sales techniques, and your expertise with the merchandise."

Tally laughed. Apparently her mother hadn't been kidding. "Upbeat sales techniques? Expertise? I don't even like Christmas."

"Pretty funny," Bonnie said, chuckling. "At least you still have your sense of humor."

"I'm serious."

"No, you're not. You loved working here."

"That's what I keep hearing."

"My God, you *are* serious."

"As a snake bite. It's starting to make me feel a little weird, too."

"Maybe if you come back to work, you'll get back to normal."

"I doubt it. We had a family dinner at my folks' place last night. The house was completely decked out for Christmas, inside and out. I could hardly wait to get away from it."

"Wow, this sounds seriouser and seriouser."

"Got any ideas for how I can get back my supposed Christmas spirit back?"

"Honest, Tally, it wasn't supposed. Other than jumping back into the fray here, I'll have to think on it."

"I appreciate that."

"Have you got a new car yet?"

"No, but I'm going to look for one tomorrow."

"Good. Maybe that will help you feel more like your old self again."

Tally doubted it. "Maybe."

"Have you seen Sam?"

"Yes…why?"

"Just wondered. He's been beside himself the entire time since the crash, especially when you didn't come out of the coma." When Tally didn't reply, she went on. "He's crazy about you, you know."

Tally let her mind wander back to the hours she and Sam had spent in her bed. "So he told me."

"He was afraid you wouldn't remember anything about him."

"My memory of him came back a bit slowly," Tally admitted, unwilling to share with Bonnie the intimate details of what had happened after that.

"I can tell from your tone that you don't want to discuss your relationship with him, and that's fine, but listen, Tally, we really do want you back at the Cottage. Call me as soon as you get your transportation issue settled and we'll set up a schedule for you, okay?"

Since she no longer had a job at Tidwell's, and she had bills to pay and no enthusiasm for job-hunting at the moment, the choice seemed obvious. "That sounds fine. Thanks for calling, Bonnie. I look forward to seeing you again."

"Me, too, sweetie. We're all so glad you're out of the coma and back with the living."

Tally disconnected and laid her phone on the table beside her house key. Her stomach rumbled, reminding her that she was hungry. At the same moment, she wondered how the Christmas clock was doing.

She wandered into the kitchen, looking for the box she'd left on the counter the night before.

It was nowhere to be seen, but the clock itself *tick-tocked* so proudly from its spot on the table, it practically had its clock face puffed out. The hands pointed straight up at the funky twelve.

If Tally hadn't been so shocked, she might have laughed. As it was, she tore the kitchen apart looking for the shoe box and all the duct tape she'd used to silence the darned thing.

Minutes later, she found the box, back on the shelf she'd taken it from.

Even more surprising was the duct tape stored in the closet at the end of the hall. Not one inch was missing from the roll.

Not. One. Inch.

Thanks to her parents, Tally had food to eat. Food that didn't have to be cooked. That was a big plus, because Tally still considered herself a novice in the kitchen. Even so, she'd been working diligently at conquering the best of her mother's recipes. Or at least, she had been, before the crash.

She opened one of those cheese-and-salami snack thingies, poured herself a glass of milk, and sat down at the little kitchen table, staring at the Christmas clock.

Why did it always point to twelve o'clock?

How did it get itself out of the duct tape, and the box?

How did the duct tape manage to get itself back on the roll?

What method of transportation had the box used to get itself back on the shelf?

Was there some kind of weird clock-and-box transporter at work in the apartment?

By the time she'd asked and pondered those questions, and more, her snack was gone. She poured another glass of milk and opened the container filled with fresh-baked chocolate chip cookies. Her mother had substituted red and green M-and-Ms for the chocolate chips, just for her.

Life is short, and then you die. Eat dessert first.

The unexpected thought was so clear, so loud, she looked around the room to make sure she was alone. When she'd ascertained it *was* from her own mind, she sat down with the milk and cookies. Alternately munching and sipping, she stared at the clock.

A whole new set of observations and questions unrelated to the clock cropped up.

Tally, admittedly, had always been an impetuous person. Still, she'd only slept with one man in her life, before last night. Did that make her an easy lay?

Or was she in love? And was being in love rationale enough for having sex with a man?

Just thinking about what she and Sam had done in her bed made her body start buzzing all over. There was nothing she wanted more than to spend the rest of her life sleeping next to him, making love with him, making babies with him. She envisioned a whole herd of little boys who looked just like their daddy, romping around the house playing fireman.

Tally grabbed another cookie, frowning.

Was she nuts?

Despite all her friends already being married, and her dreams of a fairy-tale romance, she'd never had the urge, or even given a thought to walking down the aisle, so why now?

She polished off her fifth cookie and washed it down with what remained of her milk.

Even though she was impetuous, she'd never, ever jumped into the sack with a guy on the first date…not that she and Sam had been on an actual date, and really, since she'd been the one to propose they get naked, how could she expect him not to agree?

She set the cookie container back on the counter and rinsed out her glass before placing it in the dishwasher. A glance around the kitchen told her everything was in order.

Except for the clock.

With a sigh, Tally picked it up and carried it to the living room, where she set it on the old steamer trunk she used as a coffee table. She sank down onto the sofa and spent the afternoon alternately staring out the window and studying the clock.

At dusk, which was just before five these days, the neighbors' outdoor Christmas lights popped on. Simultaneously, her phone rang. Sam's picture appeared on the screen. Tally savored looking at it for the space of two rings before she answered. "Hi."

"Hi, yourself," he said back. "How're you feeling today?"

She smiled. "Like I was well loved all night long." When he didn't respond, she thought she'd gone too far with her honesty. "Sam?"

"You take my breath away," he said.

"Is that a good thing, or a bad thing?"

"When I bring you breakfast in bed tomorrow morning, you'll have your answer."

"About that...."

"Please don't say you've been thinking and this is all a big mistake."

"I have been thinking," she admitted, "and I don't know if it's all been a big mistake, or not. It's not like me to be so forward, or to have sex with a man so soon after I've met him. In fact," she said, going for brutally honest, "I haven't slept with a man for more than five years and even then, it was only half a dozen times because I found out he had another girlfriend on the side. That was the problem with the last guy I liked, too, only he was married, but fortunately, I found that out before I slept with him." She briefly worried her bottom lip. "You don't have another girlfriend, do you Sam?"

Again, he didn't reply immediately.

Please, please, please, don't let him say yes.

"Tally, I swear to God, if it didn't mean losing my job, I'd come over there and jump your bones right now."

"I wouldn't try and stop you, but I really have to know. Do you have another girlfriend?"

"No."

Tally believed him. "What are you doing?" She was thinking maybe they could have a phone appetizer.

"I'm fixing dinner. When I'm on shift, I'm always the dinner chef."

"Making any appetizers?" she queried a bit suggestively.

"God, I wish I could," he said, his tone low and suggestive right back. "I should be able to get to your place by eight-fifteen for breakfast."

"I can hardly wait." She considered how she would greet him at the front door, but since it was over twelve hours away, she had time to finalize plans for the start to her day. "What are you fixing for dinner?"

"Polish sausages, with kraut and Swiss cheese, on rolls."

"I love sausages," she said.

"Boy, don't I know it," he said. "And on that note, my

pants are way too tight right now, and I gotta get this meal on the table."

Slightly disappointed, because she was actually enjoying their sexual repartee, Tally said, "I understand."

"Maybe I can call you later."

"Is it even possible to have a private conversation in the fire station, and by that, I mean one that includes an itty-bitty bit of sex talk?"

"If I step outside." He chuckled. "Then it could be more than an itty-bitty bit."

"You'll freeze your pecker off," she said without considering her choice of words.

Sam laughed. "It's possible, but it might be worth it, if you know what I mean."

"I think I do."

"Look, things happen around here, and if you don't hear from me, its likely because we're out on a call, so don't go getting your feelings hurt."

"I won't."

"If we do go out on a call, we might not get back at a reasonable hour, so you wouldn't hear from me until I'm on your doorstep tomorrow morning."

"I understand."

"When I bite into my polish kraut dog, I'll be thinking of you."

She giggled and disconnected before she said something else that would further delay his dinner preparations.

Moments later, she figured out exactly how she'd answer the door the next morning.

It would make breakfast in bed just that much better.

Chapter 11

Tally set her alarm for seven, but she was wide awake by six-thirty. She hopped into the shower and washed her hair, wanting to be fresh and ready for Sam.

When the doorbell sounded at 7:55 a.m., she thought he must have ditched work a little early. Just to be on the safe side, she peeked through the peep hole. Her dad stood on the other side.

Tally dashed back to her bedroom and pulled on pajamas and her robe, then hurried back to the door. "Hi, Dad."

He smiled at her. "I was hoping I wasn't too early."

"Early for what?" she asked.

"I hoped you weren't still sleeping. I thought I could take you to breakfast, then we'd go car-shopping."

Tally's spirits fell. She loved her dad, she really did, but this morning was supposed to be for Sam. Still, she didn't want to hurt her dad's feelings. "Sam is stopping by for breakfast when he gets off work." After that came the improvisation. "We're going car shopping after that."

An obvious wave of relief washed over him. "Okay, good."

"You're not upset, are you?"

"No, honey. Tessa and Jennie need help with their outdoor lights, but I told them getting you new transportation took precedence over Christmas lights. They'll be delighted when I show up to help." Just inside the door, he turned to leave.

"Dad?"

"Yeah?"

"Thank you for thinking of me."

He smiled. "You're in good hands if you're with Sam, Tally, and I think he knows more about today's cars than I do, since I'm still driving my fifty-six Chevy."

Tally grinned. "Some day, your grandkids are going to be glad you kept it." She hugged her dad and waved him off before she closed and locked the door.

Just in case someone else unexpected paid her a visit, she kept her pajamas and robe on. Once she verified it was Sam knocking, she could get back into her birthday suit.

The next fifteen minutes were some of the longest of Tally's life. She paced back-and-forth, from the door to the living room window, practically wearing a path in the carpet.

At eight-fourteen, Sam's truck pulled into her space.

Tally's heart began to pitty-patter. She raced off to her bedroom, discarded the robe and PJs, then went back to the door.

The doorbell ding-a-linged.

She peeked once more through the peep hole.

Sam. Just Sam. She unlocked the door and opened it.

It took a moment to register that the much shorter Emil Salisbury was standing beside him, though his back was turned toward Tally as he gazed toward the street. Tally gasped.

Before the door slammed, she noted that Sam's expression went from shocked to amused. All well and good for him to think her little surprise was funny. It wasn't him standing naked as a jay bird in the doorway. Through the door, she heard him belt out a laugh.

She ran to her bedroom, pulled the pajamas and her

robe on again and ran back to the front door. She took several deep breaths before she opened it.

This time, Emil faced the door. "Good morning, Mr. Salisbury," she said, avoiding looking at Sam.

"'Morning, Tally. I brought you a lasagna casserole for your dinner. I'm mighty glad you're back among the living."

Much as she appreciated his gesture, Tally would rather never hear *back among the living* again. "I am, too, Mr. Salisbury. Thank you so much for thinking of me."

"It's my pleasure. You've sure done a lot for me over the years and now it's my turn to do for you." He handed over the casserole dish, which was in a container with a handle, apparently made to carry it. "Don't worry about returning the dish right away. I hope you enjoy the lasagna." He glanced at Sam, then back at Tally with twinkling eyes. "I hear you and Fireman Sam are having breakfast together this morning." He gave her a knowing smile. "I hope you young folks enjoy that, too." He tipped the brim of the wool fedora he wore and turned to walk back down the sidewalk to his vintage 1964 Plymouth Barracuda.

Tally and Sam watched until Emil got into his cherished sports car and drove away. He'd bought the 'Cuda new and it was still in primo condition, right down to the gold paint, black leather interior, and V-8 engine. He and her dad spent a lot of time discussing classic-cars.

Sam turned to her, grinning. "You are so lucky."

"I know. I looked out the peep hole, but he's so short. I didn't see him."

Sam reached for the casserole carrier. "Let me take that and you can go back to" —he grinned again— "how you were when you opened the door the first time."

Tally handed over the carrier and hustled off to her bedroom. She was so excited about what was about to happen, she didn't give a second thought to how badly things could've gone if Emil Salisbury had been *facing* the door the first time she opened it.

Sam removed the casserole dish from the carrier and placed it in the refrigerator. Once that was done, he wandered back to the hall tree and hung up his coat. He also took off his shoes and socks and left them beside the front door.

He wasn't dressed fancy. He had on a pair of jeans that were way too tight right then, and a sweatshirt.

As he made his way down the short hallway to Tally's bedroom, he marveled that she'd taken the breakfast-in-bed proposal seriously. Certainly, he'd never expected her to show up in her birthday suit at the front door. In fact, he wouldn't be surprised if she still had on her PJs after the near-miss she'd experienced with Emil.

He paused in her doorway. She'd closed the blinds, leaving the room dusky, but not dark. A single candle burned on her dresser, flavoring the room with the scent of vanilla. A sexy instrumental played low in the background.

He stepped into the room and approached the bed. Leave it to Tally to surprise him. She was stark naked, but not stretched out in some seductive pose, crooking a finger at him. Instead, she was sitting lotus-style in the middle of the bed, chewing on her lower lip, like she had some big decision churning in that pretty head of hers.

"Tally?"

"What?" she whispered.

"You're giving me so many ideas."

"Ideas?"

He nodded, pulling off his sweatshirt and the tee shirt beneath it in one motion, letting both drop to the floor. He went next for the button on his jeans, and then the zipper, and pushed both the denim and his boxers down at the same time.

"I had no idea watching a man undress could be so sexy," she murmured.

He straightened and found her eyes glued to his erection. "And I had no idea I could be so turned on by a woman sitting cross-legged on her bed." He leaned over and did nothing more than kiss her.

He'd never kissed a woman without pulling her close or putting his arms around her. It was a unique and satisfying experience, despite the fact that no other part of them touched.

"Sam?" she said a long time later.

"What?"

"Is this wrong?"

"No."

"Are you sure? I mean…." She faltered and he straightened, staring down at her with hungry eyes. "I've thought about it and thought about it, and I want you so much it's killing me, but somehow, it seems wrong after only four days."

"Five now," he said. "Lay back and I'll show why it isn't."

She hesitated, then laid back.

"Open your legs for me."

"Why?"

"Breakfast in bed," he managed to get out, then showed her exactly what he meant.

Their time together was glorious. It might have gone on like that between them all day if the Christmas clock hadn't decided to remind them of the time at nine-thirty by blasting "Jingle Bell Rock" from it's perch on her dresser.

"What the hell?" Sam barked, rolling off of her.

"It's the Christmas clock," she said.

"The clock plays 'Jingle Bell Rock'?" he asked, staring at the dresser. "How'd it even get there? I'm sure it was on the kitchen counter when I put the lasagna in the fridge."

"It moves."

"What?"

"It moves. It also removes duct tape and escapes from shoe boxes."

He stared down at her with concern. "Are you feeling okay?"

She scooted up in the bed and leaned against the headboard. "I'm fine, but I'm not kidding you. It's some kind of magic clock."

He put a hand to her forehead, which both amused and irritated her.

"I'm fine, Sam, and I'm not making any of this up." She chewed a moment on her bottom lip, then sprang from the bed and raced to the closet at the end of the hallway outside her bedroom door. She returned with the roll of duct tape and detoured to her closet to get a shoe box. On her way back to the bed, she flicked on the light switch and grabbed the clock.

"What in the name of Christmas are you doing, Tally?"

She plopped down on the bed and emptied her arms. She held up the clock and pushed in the button on the back that silenced the music, then held the *tick-tocker* up in front of Sam's face. "Note that the hands are pointing to the twelve."

He nodded, but of course, that didn't convince him of anything.

She set the clock to the right time and proceeded to wrap it with duct tape, so the alarm button on the back couldn't pop out again. Once that was done, she placed the clock in the shoe box and taped that up as well.

"Honey, I think—"

"Don't think, Sam. I'm giving you a lesson on what this clock can do. Shall we step into the shower before we get dressed?"

She waited expectantly for his response, but none came. "I have a big shower."

"I know what you're saying, but I don't think—"

"I asked you *not* to think, Sam. You're going to have to

suspend belief in everything you know to understand this, and even then, you won't be able to make heads or tails of it." She frowned at the shoe box. "I've been living with it since Saturday night and I still don't get what's going on."

"Was the clock in the box you had in your arms the other night?"

"Yes." Without waiting for him, she made her way to the bathroom and turned on the shower.

He joined her a minute later, but it was obvious he didn't have the enthusiasm for it he might have had, if the darned clock hadn't announced itself. "Did I fall asleep at some point in the last ninety minutes?"

"No," she said, vigorously soaping herself. "And I didn't sneak out while you were *pleasuring* me to get the clock from the kitchen and put it on the dresser, either, so if you're thinking of carting me off to Grey Dixon for another neurological exam, you can forget it. There's nothing wrong with me." When he remained silent, she added, "It's all about the clock."

He stilled her hand and cupped her face with one of his. "It's okay, Tally. We'll get this figured out."

Frustrated, she shook off his hand. "I'm not crazy, Sam. I'm telling you, for real and true, this is *all* about the damned clock!"

Chapter 12

They dried and dressed without speaking. Tally was angry that Sam didn't believe her and Sam bombarded her with worried glances, no doubt thinking she was nuts.

When it was time to head out the door for the drive to After Thoughts, he picked up the shoe box and pointedly examined the tape wrapped around it.

"I get it, okay?" Tally snapped.

Despite their fantastic lovemaking, the drive downtown was made in a silence so uncomfortable, Tally considered bailing out of Sam's truck at every stop sign and stop light.

Finally, though, they arrived at After Thoughts.

Again, Sam grabbed the duct tape-wrapped shoe box and gave it another irritating once over.

"You've made your point, Mr. Reed."

He followed her into the store, where Jackie Kincannon greeted them with a smile. Evidently sensing that all was not well between the two of them, she accepted the shoe box and used a pair of scissors to cut the duct tape.

Inside the box, the stupid Christmas clock looked even more ridiculous for having duct tape triple-wrapped around it. Jackie shot a questioning glance at Tally.

Instead of trying to explain her actions, Tally merely shrugged.

Sam folded his arms over his chest and remained silent, as well.

Jackie went to work cutting off the duct tape. "I'm still not sure how the clock ended up on your doorstep, Tally, but I appreciate you bringing it back."

"It's not a problem," Tally said. "Thank you for *taking* it back."

Again, Jackie gave her a curious look. She set the clock on the counter, then gathered up the duct tape remnants and placed them inside the shoe box. "Shall I dispose of this here, or do you want it back."

"I'll take it," Tally said, glaring at the clock. "I have a feeling I'm going to need it again."

Back in Sam's truck, he said, "We're going to swing by Grey's office, and before you argue with me about it, let's just say it's a precautionary check, okay?"

"Fine," Tally huffed, though she was anything *but* fine about it.

An hour later, she smirked at Sam. "I told you everything was okay inside my head."

He nodded, but didn't look convinced. "You hungry? We never did have any *food* for breakfast, and it's almost lunchtime."

"I'm starved," she admitted, "both for you and for something to actually eat."

His head jerked in her direction. "I was afraid you'd be too pissed to make love again."

"Let's just say, I'm sex-starved where you're concerned." She kept her eyes straight ahead when she said it, afraid to see what his expression and his eyes had to say about her blatant honesty.

"So, you're not angry with me?"

"Of course, I am, but what does one have to do with the other?"

He was silent for so long, she thought he wasn't going to answer. Finally, he did. "When Missy got mad at me, she'd refuse to have sex for a week."

Tally swung her head to look at him. "You're kidding."

"I wish I was."

"I'd never do that."

"I hope that's true."

Irritated by his qualified response, she said, "Look, Sam, I'm a big girl who can have an argument and still be friends with someone."

He said nothing in reply.

"I know how to compartmentalize."

"That's not what kept me quiet."

"Then what did?"

"I thought we were more than friends."

"We are." His wounded response threw her. "Can't we be friends *and* lovers?"

"Absolutely."

"Are you going to be a problem child?"

That earned her an incredulous look.

"One thing you need to know about me, Sam, is that I speak before I think. It's a failing I've had since I learned to talk. That sometimes results in miscommunication." She pulled off a glove and reached over to stroke his cheek. "Don't ever be afraid to ask for clarification, or to speak your own mind with me."

He pulled over and shoved the gear into PARK, but left the truck running. "I have a lot to learn about you, Tally."

She grunted. "I have a lot to learn about myself, so on that point, we're even."

"I don't think I've ever met anyone who's as straight-forward as you are. It's kind of thrown me for a loop."

She found his use of *straightforward* and *forthcoming* amusing, given that he didn't believe her about the clock. Did he even realize he'd contradicted himself? "I can see that."

He stared at her for a full thirty seconds, his jaw flexing with each second.

"What are you thinking now?" she asked, almost afraid of what his reply would be.

"I was thinking, I'd like to take you straight home and have sex nonstop with you for the next two days."

Her heartbeat and the flush in her face escalated at the same, rapid rate. "That sounds good to me."

"Unfortunately, man cannot live by sex alone." He added a grin to his statement, for good measure.

"But woman, who recovers quickly, can," she retorted.

"We still have to eat."

"I'd love a polish dog," she deadpanned.

"You're killin' me."

She glanced down and noted the bulge at his groin. "Serves you right."

"Putting our minds back on *food*," he said, "what sounds good…pizza, sandwiches, soup, steak?"

"No polish?" she asked, feigning a disappointed pout.

"Later," he promised.

Tally gave him an exaggerated sigh in return. "Okay, then, I choose…pizza."

He nodded, put the truck back into DRIVE, checked for traffic, and pulled away from the curb. "What's your favorite kind?"

Tally grinned at him. "Today, I think I'll have linguicia and black olive with fresh tomatoes." She hesitated, then asked, "Did you know linguicia starts out looking like a sausage?"

After a moment of startled silence, Sam broke out laughing.

Inside Pizza Palace, they ran into Lily D'Arcy, her best friend, Jani Fridley, and Tally's sister-in-law, Sylvie.

"Where are all the kids?" Tally asked.

Lily grinned. "Sean's sister, Kat, and her husband,

Todd, have them all at PlayLand while we do some Christmas shopping."

"I suppose Kat brought her camera along," Tally said.

Lily nodded. "She thought it might be fun to do some kid photography, now that she's expecting."

"Given that she asked us to put the kids in Christmas clothes, I can hardly wait to see how this turns out," Sylvie said. "You guys want to join us?"

"Sure," Sam said.

"Chicken," Tally whispered to him when he helped her out of her coat.

He grinned.

"I should be going," Jani said.

"Don't," Tally pleaded, putting a hand on Jani's arm. After a moment's hesitation, she said, "I'm really sorry about you and Jim, Jani, and what happened to him."

Sam reached under the table and gave her thigh a squeeze.

Tally didn't know if he was offering support or warning her to tread lightly.

Jani sank back down in her chair. "It's me who's sorry for what he did to you."

Tally said with all earnesty, "Jim was his own man, wasn't he? What happened wasn't your fault any more than it was mine."

Jani's eyes teared up. "I get angry every time I think about him drinking and driving, hitting your car...."

"I'm fine," Tally assured her. She glanced at Sam, then back at Jani. "The neurologist says I'm back to normal, which may or may not be a good thing."

That got chuckles out of the others and Sam relaxed enough to head to the counter to order pizza and soft drinks.

"When is Kat due?" Tally asked Lily.

"May. They're hoping for twins so they can stop at two."

"Good luck with that," said Jani, who was CFO for D'Arcy Implements. "It didn't work for you."

"I love having four kids," Lily said, "and despite my previous feelings on the subject, having one more is going to be the icing on the cake."

"You're pregnant?" Tally cried.

"Just barely," Lily admitted. "I didn't even mean to say it, but the words just came out."

Tally reached over and hugged her. "You're a lucky woman, Lily."

"Don't I know it, and Sean's excited about it, but worried we're outgrowing the house."

"You have a big lot," Sylvie said. "You could add on."

"That's what I told him, because I love our neighborhood." She grinned. "He'll come around eventually, but for the moment, he's contemplating other digs."

"Men," the three women across from Tally murmured in unison.

A moment later, Sam came back carrying a tray of soft drinks. "What?" he asked, when they snickered.

"Nothing," Lily said. "Just girl humor." She glanced at Jani and Sylvie. "We should get going, if we want to shop more before we have to meet Kat and Todd."

Minutes later, Tally and Sam were alone, exchanging heated glances.

"I need to make two stops before we head to my place," he said.

"Your place?" she asked. "What's wrong with my place?"

"Nothing love, but I have a king-sized bed and you don't."

Chapter 13

Sam's first stop was the Gingerbread Cottage. Bonnie greeted Tally with tears and hugs. Zoë Manning, working at the FruityCakes counter, went to the kitchen to find Stevie and Charley, who came rushing in with more tears and hugs.

Sam stood beside Bonnie's husband, Griff, and took it all in.

"Are you ready to come back to work?" Charley asked.

Tally glanced around at all the Christmas merchandise. Now that she was in the thick of it, it didn't seem quite so overwhelming. "Maybe."

"Oh, I hope so," Stevie said. "Bonnie's due any minute, you know, and she doesn't have her usual boundless energy."

Tally couldn't believe she hadn't noticed Bonnie was pregnant, but she glanced down at her belly, and there it was, a big baby bump, hidden behind a Gingerbread Cottage apron. "Congratulations! I feel like an idiot. I didn't even notice you're expecting."

"Easy to miss behind this gargantuan apron Granny made me," Bonnie said with a laugh. She shot a look at her husband, who winked back at her.

"That's Granny for you," Charley said.

"No kidding," Stevie agreed. "I wonder if she was thinking everyone who works here is going to give birth to triplets."

"God, I hope not," Griff said, feigning distress.

Bonnie walked over and slid her arms around his middle. "Don't worry, sweetie. We're going to get ours one at a time."

With that reassurance, he leaned down and kissed her with so much passion, Tally said, "Get a room, why don't you."

Griff ignored her and carried on with his kiss.

"When can you start back?" Charley asked.

"I'm going car shopping this afternoon…." She thought about the plans she had with Sam. "Or maybe tomorrow. What about Friday?"

Stevie glanced at Bonnie. "You think you'll make it that long?"

"I have Tally on speed dial. Whether she has a car or not, she can be here. Someone will give her a ride, right, Sam?"

"You can count on me to set her up with a ride pool," Sam said.

"Thank God for firefighters," Tally said with her tongue firmly planted in her cheek.

Sam shot her one of his searing glances, which she returned in kind. "It was really good to see all of you, but we need to take off now. I have lots to catch up on."

Five minutes later, carrying a delicious FruityCake, they climbed into Sam's truck and headed toward his house.

They made the second stop along the way.

Tally wasn't sure how she felt about using condoms at this stage of the game, but on the other hand, she also didn't know if she was ready to be a mom.

Sam pulled the truck into his garage and lowered the door.

Tally started peeling off her clothes before he came around to help her climb out.

Sam remembered to grab the FruityCake and followed her inside the house.

Between the two of them, they left a trail of clothing, undergarments, shoes, and socks all the way to his bedroom.

"I thought we were never going to get here," he murmured against her breast.

"You're the one who added the extra stops," she reminded him, then uttered a moan of pleasure as he slid his hand between them. "I'm so ready for you. Don't make me wait."

With that tiny bit of urging, he found the moist spot between her legs and thrust into her.

Two hours later, Sam said, "I'm hungry. What would you like for dinner?"

Too sated with spent passion to move, Tally threw him a curve ball. "You?"

"Tally, love, you've exhausted me. I need some sustenance to get me going again, before, well, you know."

She did know and it made her grin. "Methinks thou dost protest too much." She reached for his package, but he climbed out of the bed before her hand could connect with his family jewels.

"You don't have to get up," he said, staring down at her.

"But you are," she said, her eyes on his groin. "And you thought you were done."

Sam looked down in surprise.

"How'd you miss it?" she asked, moving toward him.

Looking baffled, he said, "I have no idea. I guess dinner can wait for a bit."

Tally smiled and pulled him down on top of her.

An hour later, they sat in front of his fireplace, naked, eating peanut butter and jelly sandwiches and Cheetos.

"I've never tasted anything so good," Tally said, licking her orange fingertips.

Sam, his eyes glued to what she was doing, said, "It's the sex. It affects how food tastes."

She glanced at him, wide eyed. "It does?"

"Stop looking at me like that."

"Like what?"

"Like I'm dessert."

"But you *are* dessert."

"I beg to differ. *You're* dessert."

"Can't we both be dessert?"

He gave her a sly smile. "I like the way you think."

"I like the way *you* think, too." She placed her paper plate and napkin on the coffee table. "That thing you did with your fingers…."

"Yes?"

"Would you like to try that on my, um, you know, again?"

"Gladly."

Several hours later, they moved back to the bedroom and around two a.m., both fell into a deep sleep.

Tally woke first. It was still dark outside, but the digital clock claimed it was seven a.m. She tiptoed to the window and had a peek through the blinds. It was snowing again.

From there, she went to the bathroom, then ventured to the kitchen to see what Sam had in the fridge. It was well-stocked, which was no surprise. As the designated cook when he was on firefighter duty, it only stood to reason that he'd keep his own larder supplied.

After a thorough examination, Tally decided on a ham-and-cheese scramble with cinnamon-raisin English muffins and sliced bananas on the side. Simple enough for even her to handle, but it didn't feel quite right to fix breakfast in her birthday suit.

She crept back to the bedroom intent on finding Sam's

tee shirt to slip into, when it dawned on her that the trail of discarded clothing no longer littered the path from the garage door to his bedroom. Curious about when he'd picked up the clothes, she wondered what he'd done with them. If she turned on the light, it would surely disturb him, and really, he'd been so passionate all night long, he had to be exhausted. She didn't want to waken him just so she could cover herself.

Instead, she tiptoed over to his dresser and found the tee shirt drawer. She pulled one out, then tiptoed back out of his bedroom and made her way to the kitchen again.

Outside, even though it was snowing, the day had begun to lighten. The dusky light filtered through the window coverings. Since she was now sort of dressed, she made her way around the house, opening them.

Back in the kitchen, she put on a pot of coffee, then gathered everything she needed to make breakfast. She decided to let Sam sleep until eight, then she'd wake him up in the best possible way, and after that, they'd have their breakfast.

Satisfied with her plan, she poured herself a cup of coffee and went to the living room, where she turned on the fireplace and snuggled under a blanket to watch the mammoth snowflakes fall.

Sam cursed himself up one side and down the other. Just because a friend had texted and asked for an assist didn't mean he always had to go running.

He could have stayed in bed with Tally until he had to report in for work tomorrow morning, but no. He was at the bottom of a ravine with a dead phone and no freaking way to get up the cliff to the road again, unless he sprouted wings.

He turned and glanced at the truck. Only God knew how he'd survived going over the hundred-foot drop. He hadn't landed hood-first in the river, either, but with all four wheels on the ground, and a good ten feet from the icy current. Miracle number two.

He was glad he'd had the foresight to leave Tally a note after the three a.m. text had come in from Ryker Manning about the reindeer. The ultimate irony concerning the predicament he was in now was that he'd swerved off the road trying to avoid *hitting* a damned reindeer. Was it part of the herd Ryker was reindeer-sitting for the Kringles? Or was it a stray reindeer from who knew where? If only he could get cell reception, so he could call for help.

That made him wonder if Ryker thought he'd crapped out on him. Maybe his responding text when he'd torn himself away from Tally's warm, luscious body had said something different than *OK* to his friend.

His head hurt so bad, Sam wasn't really sure now that he'd responded to Ryker at all. Maybe he'd dreamed that, or maybe Ryker was out looking for him now, or maybe Ryker had come knocking on his door and found Tally instead and the two of them....

He put the skids to his imagination so fast on that last thought, he almost got whiplash.

Ryker wouldn't do that to him, and neither would Tally. The lump on the side of his head was making him think crazy thoughts. He didn't even know how long he'd been unconscious before he'd awakened and climbed out of the truck.

He went back to his truck and tilted his head back, studying the hillside again. There *had* to be a way up.

Maybe when the cloud cover broke, he'd be able to see better, and figure it out.

Chapter 14

When Tally woke again, she was surprised to note by the clock on the DVR that it was 10:30. How had that happened, and why hadn't Sam woken her?

She threw back the blanket and made her way to his bedroom. Again on tiptoes, she approached his side of the bed, but there was no Sam there. Surprised, she checked the bathroom. Also empty. She called out his name, but no answer. Stymied, she stuck her head in every room on her way to the kitchen. Still no Sam.

At that point, she decided he must be in the garage. She pulled open the door, but the garage was empty of both Sam and his truck. What the heck? Where would he go and why hadn't he told her he was leaving?

Slightly miffed, she put away all the breakfast fixings and returned to his bedroom. She thought about making the bed, decided against it, then because she never left her own bedroom with an unmade bed, tackled the job, letting her pique spur her on. Next, she jumped into the shower, and after that, her clothes. Still no Sam.

She picked up her phone and called the fire station.

No one answered, which told Tally the firefighters must be out on a call.

By then, worry began to mix in with her irritation. Where could he have gone?

She waited another hour, but he never showed up.

Tally picked up her phone again and called for an Uber, only to be told that no transportation was available due to the storm.

Really irked now, she disconnected and dialed her brother, Micah.

"He's out on the snowplow," Sylvie said. "Want me to call him and see if he can come pick you up?"

"I'd appreciate it," Tally said. "Thanks."

Five minutes later, her phone rang. Sylvie said, "Micah's on his way to get you."

"Great. I'll wait outside for him."

"Tally?"

"Yeah?"

"Where's Sam?"

"Honestly? I have no idea."

"How did you get to his place?"

"With Sam, but I still have no idea where he is now."

"That's peculiar."

"Tell me about it."

"I hope he's okay."

Tally thought about the hours she'd spent making love with him, and how tireless he'd been. "He's in really good shape, so I'm sure he's fine." When Sylvie didn't reply, she asked, "Do you know something I don't?"

"I wish I did, then you'd know where he is."

"I hear the snowplow now. Catch'ya later, and thanks again."

"You're welcome. Call me when you hear from Sam."

Tally responded with a garbled sound that could have meant anything. She disconnected and quickly pulled on her coat, scarf, and gloves. She wished like crazy that she had her snow boots, then she could have walked home, but *c'est la vie* on that. It would be warm in the cab of the snowplow and Micah would have her home much quicker.

Tally had no idea how to deal with the deadbolt on

Sam's front door, so she left it unlocked. By the time she reached the curb, Micah was slowing to a stop.

He opened the door and offered her a hand up. "Where's Sam?"

"I have no idea."

"You two have a spiff?"

"Not that I know of."

"Then why don't you know where he is?"

"You tell me. He says you've gotten to be really good friends over the past year."

"I haven't heard a word from him." Micah frowned. "Did you try the firehouse?"

"No answer."

"Curious."

"Maybe so, but it's too early to call in the cops," she said, half-joking.

Micah's glance went to the driveway. "I don't see any tire tracks." He looked back at her. "Did you check the garage?"

"Of course! Do I look like an idiot?"

Instead of grinning, like he usually would, Micah glanced once more toward Sam's house. "It isn't like Sam to take off without saying something. Did he leave you a note?"

"He left me jack shit, okay? No note, no text message, no voicemail, no sexy love words in my ear."

Micah opened his mouth, then snapped it shut. He'd never been worth a damn when it came to tears, and dammit, she did have tears. Ten minutes later, he dropped her off at her place.

Too emotional to give him a hug, she mumbled, "Thanks," and jumped out of the cab. Once inside her apartment, she went around closing all the window coverings.

She needed peace and quiet and privacy to do some serious thinking about a man who had proved himself a sex god in bed, then turned around and left without saying one word to her about where he was going, or what he was doing, or why he'd left her all alone.

Her stomach rumbled, reminding her that she hadn't made that ham-and-cheese scramble. Uncaring what she shoved into her mouth, she put on a pot of coffee, then grabbed two packs of green Hostess Sno Balls and two packs of Twinkies. *Thank you, Mom.*

Twenty minutes later, gorging on almost straight sugar while she sipped her coffee, she realized she hadn't checked her phone for voicemails or text messages.

She jumped up to retrieve it, disappointed when she had neither.

She went back to wondering exactly what had happened, giving her insecurities an invite to mess with her head. Had Sam just been using her for a convenient lay? Was that all she was to him?

Good, lord, could she really be that bad at reading people?

Well, what did she expect? Hadn't she had misgivings about having sex with him after only knowing him for four days? Served her right if he did take off without so much as a goodbye! The only thing not typical about the way he'd done it was that he'd obviously taken off while she was still in his bed, and before it had started to snow again. She hadn't even thought to check out the driveway until Micah made the comment about no tire tracks in the snow.

That's when her thoughts turned south.

Until that moment, she'd really thought Sam had ditched her in the worst possible way, but what if he hadn't? What if something else was going on?

In a real funk by then, she cleaned up her breakfast-slash-lunch wrappers and shuffled off to her bedroom. There, she stared at the bed where she and Sam had experienced the most amazing hours together. A tear slid down her cheek. "Amazing, my ass," she muttered.

Tally wanted nothing more than to curl up in that bed and die, but on second thought, she'd have to *be* dead to climb back under those covers again, where the smell of him lingered to taunt her.

She might have stood there staring at her bed for the rest of the day, but an unexpected intrusion, dragged her from her reverie.

Even though she'd half-expected the reappearance, she whirled, screaming, "How did you get back here?"

The Christmas clock's only response was to keep playing "Jingle Bell Rock," which infuriated her to no end.

Tally stormed over to the insufferable clock and pressed the button on the back to silence it. As usual, both hands spun around the clock face before landing on the twelve. Depending on how she looked at it, the idiotic clock was either an hour slow, or eleven hours fast.

She contemplated throwing it against the wall, but that wouldn't serve any purpose, except to damage the wall, which her landlord wouldn't appreciate. Wrapping it up with duct tape obviously had no effect on it, either, nor did securing it inside a duct-taped shoe box.

Tally threw up her arms in disgust. Screw the clock. She had more important things on her mind.

She whirled away and in a fit of fury, yanked the comforter and both blankets off the bed. She briefly considered shredding the sheets, but since she only had one set, she ripped them off the bed, instead, and took them to the washer. She dumped in a lid full of liquid detergent, and for good measure, a scoop of OxyClean. That oughta take care of any Sam-scent he'd left behind.

As soon as the washer began to agitate, she regretted throwing the sheets in the machine to obliterate Sam's scent.

An hour later, wallowing in misery, Tally realized she'd never been a wallower in her life. She was a happy-go-lucky woman, with a good mind, even though she apparently was not good at choosing men.

Keeping the positive aspect of that in mind, she perked up a bit. Wallowing aside, what could she do about the troubling, non-positive piece?

Granted her thirtieth birthday loomed just weeks away,

but that didn't mean she'd be kissing her youth goodbye.

She was also surrounded by people who loved her. It was obvious from what she'd learned from her parents and Micah, many of those she knew had stepped forward to help take care of her and exercise her limbs while she'd been in the coma. Those same people had also been there for her family, which had been a blessing.

All told, it made her wonder why Sam had hung around waiting for her to come out of the coma, if all he wanted to do was screw her, then take off for parts unknown when he was done with her. It didn't make sense.

In her nightclothes by then, Tally threw the sheets into the dryer, then turned to prowling her apartment. All she could think of was Sam, Sam, Sam.

Her and Sam, kissing, touching, participating in the most intimate contact two people could share. Whispering love words to each other. Heck, he'd even asked her to marry him, which she still suspected was a proposal made in jest. Still, she'd halfway hoped it was real. To discover it probably wasn't, cut her to the quick.

The dryer buzzed. She fetched the sheets and made her bed, then crawled under the covers and cried herself to sleep.

If only she could make up her mind which side of the fence she was on concerning Sam's mysterious disappearance.

Tally awoke to sunny skies and a sunnier outlook. She considered staying in bed all day, but what would that solve?

She had no man. She had no plans. She also had no car. She didn't have her dog back, either, and Buttercup would have at least been a sounding board who listened to her whine without comment.

What she did have, though, was a brain, and her brain was telling her something was wrong.

Yes, she'd been ticked when she thought Sam had cut out on her, but everyone deserved a second chance. Call her a naïve fool, but that was her perspective and she was sticking with it.

She dragged herself out of bed and took a shower. Ignoring protests from her pity-party self, she got dressed and called her dad. "Can you take me car shopping?"

"Sure, honey," Bryan said, "but I thought Sam took you yesterday."

"It didn't work out, schedule-wise," she said, hoping her tone didn't say otherwise.

"Can we go around ten?"

"Ten is perfect. I'll meet you at the curb."

"Sounds good. Mom and I are in the middle of battling a pesky string of lights on the tree that keep going out, so I probably can't make it earlier."

"I thought you were going to get a new pre-lit tree this year."

"That was last Christmas, and we kinda had other things on our mind."

How could she have forgotten that she'd taken up space in a lot of people's heads over the past year?

"You okay, Tally?"

"Yeah, why?"

"You sound a little down."

"Only because I don't have a car," she ad libbed. Next, she called Bonnie at Gingerbread Cottage. "I hope you aren't giving birth today, because I haven't got a car yet."

"You're in luck. I have it on good authority that I have at least a week to go. When do you think you *will* have a car?"

"My dad's taking me out today. My goal is to drive myself home in a brand new ride no later than four o'clock."

"Such precision," Bonnie teased.

"Yeah, that's me. Good ole precise Tally."

"You sure you're okay?"

How many times would she have to answer that question? "Honest, I'm fine. I'll call and give you an update on my availability later."

"Perfect. How's Sam?"

"Gotta go. My dad's here." A small lie, and one that made Tally cringe, because she wasn't a liar.

The *How's Sam?* question ranked right up there with queries she didn't want to hear one more time. It would be bad enough, working side-by-side with Bonnie, who was good friends with Sam. She was sure to dig deeper into how things were progressing between the two of them.

Since Tally had an hour to kill, she opened her laptop and did some research on cars. At five before ten, she pulled on her snow boots, then picked up her phone again and hit Sam's number.

Second chance, Sam. Pick up.

But he didn't. In fact, the call went to voicemail after the first ring. Either his phone was off, or it was out of battery.

Second chance re-do.

She dialed the fire station. This time someone answered, but when she asked to speak to Sam, she was told that he'd switched shifts and wouldn't be in until Friday.

Being a firefighter, Sam was prepared for anything, or so he thought. He had a stash of candy bars in his glove box, a six-pack of water tucked behind the driver's seat, and spare batteries in the console for his Maglite. He also had a bottle of ibuprofen stashed there—he'd already taken more than he cared to count to ease the pounding in his head—and two blankets, along with a first-aid kit, which contained a waterproof container of matches.

What he didn't have was a newspaper or any dry wood to start a fire. Some Boy Scout-turned soldier-turned fireman he was! If he ever got up that hillside, he'd have a valuable lesson behind him. One learned the hard way.

At least the sun was shining, which should help make up for the fact that he didn't have a rope, either.

Feeling a little deflated, Tally pulled on her coat, a knit cap, and her gloves. She shoved her phone into her purse, remembered to turn off the coffee maker, and let herself out. Her dad pulled up at the curb exactly when he said he would.

"I know this is going to sound strange, Dad, but I think Sam is missing."

Her father, in the process of shoving the gear of his truck back into DRIVE, turned to her with a startled expression. "That deserves a little more explanation."

It felt a little awkward to be telling her dad that she'd spent the night at Sam's place, but she managed to choke it out.

To his credit, he didn't give her the evil eye, or a lecture. "Okay, but what leads you to think he's missing?"

"He wasn't there when I woke up, and he didn't leave a note or anything."

"How long did you wait for him?"

"Quite a while. I also called the fire station, but no one answered. Micah came to get me in the snowplow and gave me a ride home."

"At least you didn't try to walk home in this weather. Have you tried calling Sam?"

She nodded. "His phone goes straight to voice mail. I also called the station. They said he'd switched shifts and wouldn't be in until tomorrow."

"That seems to indicate he's been in contact with them."

"I know. I should have asked when he made that swap." Misery threatened to take over again. "It doesn't feel right that he left me without so much as a goodbye kiss."

Her father favored her with a frown, which told her not to go anywhere near mentioning her sleepover details again.

"I need you to do me another favor," Tally said.

"Name it," Bryan said.

"Can we take a run by Sam's place, see if maybe he's there now?"

"I don't see why not." He pulled away from the curb, and within ten minutes, they parked in front of Sam's house. "No tire tracks in the driveway."

That didn't bode well for him being there. "His front door has a deadbolt, and I didn't have a key to lock it."

"You left his house unlocked?"

"I didn't know what else to do." She frowned. "I guess I could've gone out through the garage."

Her father scowled at that option.

"Maybe I could've beat the garage door coming down."

"That sounds like a hare-brained idea." He shut off the truck. "Since we're here, we might as well check inside."

They crunched their way through the snow to the front door. Bryan knocked, but no one answered. He tried the knob and the door opened. He stepped inside and called out, "Sam, it's Bryan!"

There was no response.

"Maybe he has a spare key somewhere."

"He has a key rack by the door going into the garage," her father said. "First, though, let's take a walk through the house."

All the looking in the world wasn't going to make Sam appear, but Tally agreed. Her dad, however, found a piece of paper sticking out from beneath the bed. He scanned it quickly and handed it over to her.

With trembling fingers, Tally took it. *Tally, a friend texted me that he needs help. Make yourself at home. Should be home around noon. Love, Sam.*

She glanced at her father. "I thought he went off without telling me."

"Sam's not that kind of man," Bryan said.

Feeling terrible for doubting Sam, Tally felt even worse when she caught the note of censure in her dad's tone. Why didn't she have the faith in Sam that her family had?

They ended up at the garage, where her dad opened the

door and checked to make sure Sam's truck was, indeed, gone. He studied the key rack. "This is it." He handed it to her. "Don't lose it."

"I won't, but wouldn't you rather keep it?"

"I'm not the one having a relationship with him."

"Are you mad at me about that, Dad?"

"No, I think Sam will make a fine son-in-law."

"Uh, did he say something to you?"

"He mentioned a Christmas wedding." Almost as an afterthought, he added, "Which is more than Mom and I heard from you."

"Um...." Maybe his proposal *had* been serious. "Do you think we should check and see if he's been admitted to the hospital?"

"Good idea." He pulled out his phone.

"You have the hospital on speed dial?"

He gave her a look. "I never deleted the number after they released you to our care." A moment later, he said, "This is Bryan Barrow. Can you tell me if you've had any recent accident victims brought in? ... What about Sam Reed? Has he been admitted? ... Okay, thanks for checking." He disconnected and said to Tally, "Not there."

"Should we report him as a missing person?"

"Doesn't Micah have a friend who's a cop?"

She nodded. "Jake Rendow." She whipped out her phone and made the call. "Hi, Jakey, it's Tally. ... No, I'm doing well, thanks. Look, Sam has disappeared. Is there some time limit about reporting a missing person?" She glanced at her watch. "About thirty-six hours. ... Okay, I will. Thanks." She put her phone away and said to her dad, "Jakey says they can take a report at forty-eight hours, but he can still start looking on his own. Do we have time to stop by the fire station?"

"Honey, it's your car-shopping trip. We can stop as many places as you like."

Chapter 15

Tally hesitated in the living room. "You know, I'm pretty sure I turned off the coffee maker yesterday, but let me give it a quick check."

Bryan nodded and headed for the front door.

In the kitchen, no one was more surprised than Tally when she noticed the Christmas clock on Sam's counter, ticking away, both hands pointed to twelve o'clock. She gave the coffee maker a quick look-see then turned and left the kitchen.

She'd worry about the clock later. Besides, she wasn't even sure she'd seen what she thought she'd seen in the kitchen. As she hustled to the front door, she did know one thing, the clock seemed to have a mind of its own. Either that, or her mind that was off kilter, playing tricks on her. She didn't know which possibility frightened her more.

As if to confirm the matter, the strains of "Jingle Bell Rock" filled her ears. She slammed the front door behind her and turned the key in the deadbolt lock.

Her father gave her a funny look when she rushed down the sidewalk to the curb. "Everything okay?"

"Yep. The coffee maker was off."

"Why were you running like the hounds of hell were after you?"

"Was I? I guess I'm just cold."

That answer seemed to appease him as he drove on to their next stop. Sam's fire station would have only been five minutes from his house on non-snowy roads. Today, it took them twelve minutes to get there.

Inside, Tally introduced herself to the person manning the short counter in the tiny entrance way.

Timmy Kincannon introduced himself back.

"Are you related to Jackie?" she asked.

"Sure am," he said with a grin. "She's been my sweetheart for over ten years."

Small world. Christmas clock. After Thoughts. Jackie, who hadn't sold it, and now Timmy, her husband, who worked with Sam.

Timmy extended a hand to both of them with a big smile. "And you're the woman Sam's gonna marry. Nice to meet you, Tally. What can I do for you?"

"I'm looking for Sam."

"He's not working today, but he'll be back on tomorrow." His expression registered his puzzlement. "Since you're his fiancée, shouldn't you know where he is?"

Tally tried to make light of the question. "You'd think, huh?" She exchanged a glance with her father, who gave her a nod of encouragement. "I'd like to talk to whomever he spoke to about the shift switch."

"That would be me. Jackie needed some heavy lifting at the store tomorrow, so Sam agreed to switch shifts with me, so I could help her."

"Did he seem okay when you saw him?"

"I didn't actually *see* him. I texted him and he texted me back." He frowned. "Why all the questions?"

"I think Sam is missing."

"That can't be right. I sent the text Tuesday night and his reply was in my inbox when I got up Wednesday morning. Why do you think he's missing? When did you see him last?"

Tally didn't like sharing her personal life with a virtual stranger, especially since she didn't know if he'd spread the information around the entire fire department. "Early Wednesday morning." She gnawed her lower lip. "Can you think of anybody he might have contacted, or who might have contacted him, that I might talk to?"

"Only the guys here." He put two fingers into his mouth and let out an ear-splitting whistle. Moments later, four other men crowded into the small space. "Guys, this is Sam's girl."

"I remember you," one of the men said. "You decorated for us last year. My wife was completely jealous that the fire station looked better than our house."

The other firefighters laughed and agreed.

"Tally thinks Sam is missing. Any of you mugs seen or talked to him?"

They all shook their heads and replied in the negative.

"I'm Tally's dad, Bryan," her father said. "I've met some of you, so you know what we've gone through over the past year. If Sam's in some kind of trouble, and you know about it, we'd really like to help him."

"Sam's a straight shooter, Bryan," said Timmy. "He doesn't smoke or gamble or do drugs, and he drinks in moderation, so I can't think of any trouble he might have got himself into like that."

The other firefighters nodded their agreement. "We can start making some calls though," one of them said. "Leave us your number, in case we hear anything."

"Thank you," Tally said. She recited her number to Timmy, who wrote it down. "I appreciate your help."

"We're more than happy to give it," Timmy said, "and we're also glad you've made a full recovery."

Tally smiled, but if her recovery had gone so well, why did she keep seeing a Christmas clock that couldn't possibly be there because she'd taken it back to After Thoughts?

"Where to next?" her dad asked when they were in his truck again.

"The Fiat dealership. With any luck, they have exactly the car I want, at a price I can afford."

Tally had never liked car-shopping. For one thing, she didn't like haggling. She knew how much money she had, how much she could afford for her monthly payment, and a pretty good idea of how much her insurance would be every month. Of course, all that was based on having a fulltime, good-paying job, not a part-time position at Gingerbread Cottage.

With the test drive complete, her dad did an inspection of the engine, asking lots of questions as he went.

Being a slow day at the dealership because of the weather, the salesman seemed happy to answer all his queries. Being a slow day at the dealership, the salesman also didn't seem inclined to wiggle on the price. He firmly resisted one penny less than the MSRP.

After five minutes, Tally stood up and said, "Thanks for your time." She headed for the door.

Fred-the-sales-guy jumped up. "Wait! Where are you going?"

"To look at other dealerships."

"But I thought you loved this Fiat."

"I do, but I can't pay the price you're asking, and even if I could, I know from doing research on the Internet that you're gouging me to the tune of five-K. That's just not acceptable."

Fred did a pretty good imitation of a fish out of water. "Let me go talk to the manager."

"How long will that take?"

"Uh, twenty, thirty minutes."

"I'll give you five, as a courtesy. More than that and I'm outta here."

"But I've spent almost two hours with you."

"And apparently, I've wasted the same amount of time with you."

He stalked off in a huff to find his manager.

"I'm guessing you have a backup plan," her father said.

"Not really. I hope he'll come back and take my offer, but if not, I know exactly what I want now, so I suppose I could order it online and have it delivered."

"How long does that take, if it's even possible?"

"Oh, it's possible. I checked it out this morning while I was doing research on the Fiat. I could probably have it by Monday."

"Wow. I'm taking you with me next time I buy a car."

"Don't be so impressed with my negotiating skills. I haven't got my Fiat yet." Five minutes later, Tally said to her dad, "Let's go."

They were at the double-glass doors when someone yelled, "Wait!" across the display room.

Tally turned, expecting Fred, but it wasn't Fred. It was a man about her dad's age. He introduced himself with a handshake and a grin "I'm impressed you got to Fred. Let's get this contract written up, shall we?"

An hour later, paperwork signed, keys in-hand, and the price fifteen hundred less than she'd expected, Tally climbed into her new car. The Fiat 500L Lounge had a red body, a black top, and a red-and-black leather interior. It sat five and had a cargo space at the rear, plus satellite radio, which was free for the first three months. It felt way more substantial than her totaled VW and it drove like a jewel. "Thanks, Dad."

"You're welcome, honey, but I should be thanking you. I had no idea it was possible to get more money off a vehicle than you'd asked for originally. I feel like I've been fleeced all these years."

"It's all in the mindset. You have to be willing to walk away if you don't get what you want." She smirked at him. "How long since you actually bought a new car?"

"Uh, twenty years?" He leaned down and gave her a quick kiss. "Where are you going next?"

"I thought I'd take a drive out to Gingerbread Cottage, see how she does for the distance."

He tapped the top of the little SUV. "Drive safe and watch out for drunk drivers."

She glanced up at him with a serious expression. "You know I will."

He nodded, as if satisfied, then backed away from the Fiat and watched as she made her way out of the lot and onto the snow-packed street.

Tally pulled over at the first gas station. While she waited for her tank to fill, which didn't taken long because it was almost full, she paired her iPhone with the Bluetooth. Everything else was manageable, and if Sam ever rode with her, she felt that he'd be comfortable, despite his size.

Before her crash, she never would've chosen a red vehicle, but now, it seemed prudent to have a car that would stand out, whether against the snow or the landscape.

She paid for the gas, eased back onto the roadway, and headed north.

Along the way, she wondered where Sam was. One of the reasons she wanted to talk to Bonnie in person was to pick her brain for a list of Sam's friends. She intended to call each and every one of them on the off chance they'd know, or at the very least, could point her in the direction of someone who did.

It began to snow again before she reached the turnoff that lead to FruityCakes and Gingerbread Cottage.

So much for sunshine.

Despite her earlier expectations, her hopes that she'd find Sam took a little nosedive.

Chapter 16

Sam spent a frustrating hour trying to make his way up the hillside before it started snowing again. He'd known it would be a futile attempt, but he had to try, anyway.

Finally, he gave up and went back to the truck. He'd checked it over for fuel leaks the day before, and found none, so he felt comfortable turning on the engine for a few minutes to warm up.

As luck would have it, both the headlights and the tail-lights had been damaged on the rough ride down the side of the cliff. That begged the question of how *he* had managed to survive pretty much unscathed, if you didn't count the bump on his head, or the mammoth headache. The only explanation he could come up with remained the same. He'd been blessed with a miracle.

He opened a Baby Ruth, broke it in half, and folded the wrapper back around, to save the other half for later.

Sam rarely got angry, but he was thoroughly pissed that it was snowing again. They'd had snow on the ground in the valley since Thanksgiving. That was a freaking week ago. Enough was enough, even for a guy who liked the white stuff.

As the day grew dark, he settled in under one of his blankets and let his mind wander to Tally.

What was she doing?

Had she been angry when she'd found his note, or was she worried about him?

Had she bought a new car yet?

Was she already planning their wedding, or had she decided she didn't want to marry a man who cut out in the middle of the night to help a friend, without so much as a goodbye kiss?

With that thought came another. Had Ryker sent out a search party for him yet? He was convinced at this point that his *OK* hadn't communicated that he was on his way. Ryker most likely thought he'd blown him off.

That troubled him. Ryker Manning was a great guy. He'd served as an Army Ranger, then come home and helped his dad with the family ranch. Not too long after, his parents, Kip and Irene Manning, had relocated to Arizona. They'd given the ranch to Ryker and his sister, Zoë, but Zoë wasn't big on living the ranch life. Ryker had bought out her share, though Zoë was living there temporarily while she looked for a new place in town.

Ryker had also become an ordained minister, something he'd undertaken to give spiritual solace to his brothers and sisters in arms. To date, he'd officiated at many of his friends' weddings at the Christmas Valley Inn. Sam had already asked him to perform his and Tally's ceremony. Ryker had agreed.

Shivering slightly, Sam pulled the other blanket up over him and finally dozed off, dreaming of the woman he loved.

Dinner at the Conte home was delicious. Griff fussed over Bonnie, whose belly was testing the confines of the Christmas maternity top Granny had made for her.

Bonnie's two girls, Sadie and Casey, were perfect little

rapscallions, darting off to the Christmas tree after dinner to see if any new presents might have arrived that they hadn't yet noticed. They came squealing back and threw their arms around Tally.

"Thank you!" they cried in unison.

Tally had spent a short time talking to Bonnie at the Cottage. It was so busy, she chipped in to help, then accepted Bonnie's invite to join her family for dinner. She promised to give Tally a list of Sam's friends after they ate.

So here they were. Griff, in his Christmas apron, also made by Granny, and four females, watching him. He'd not only prepared the meal, but he was cleaning up, too.

Tally had to turn away when he stopped at the table after the dishes were done to plant a long, passionate kiss on his wife. It reminded her too much of what she and Sam had spent hours doing before he'd disappeared.

"I'll get the movie going for the girls, then I'll be back," he said to them.

"Thanks, honey," Bonnie said, her face flushed. "God, I love that man," she said when he'd left the kitchen.

"He's going to help you make a list of Sam's friends?" Tally asked.

"Griff is an investigator. He's going to help us *find* Sam."

"He is?" Tally bit her bottom lip. "I'm afraid I'm not in great financial straits at the moment. Does he take payments on time?"

Bonnie grinned. "For you and me, he works for free."

"Boy, do I," Griff said from the doorway, affecting a beleaguered posture.

Bonnie's grin morphed into a delighted laugh. "You are so downtrodden, you poor thing."

They shared an eye contact that was so laden with love and desire, it almost hurt to watch them.

Bonnie patted the seat next to her. "Shall we get started?"

Griff nodded, but took the chair opposite his wife. "I

don't want to embarrass Tally, if I feel compelled to man-handle you while she's here. Sitting over here will help preserve both our reputations."

Bonnie mouthed, *I love you*, to him and he mouthed back, *I love you, too.*

Tally thought for a minute, despite Griff taking a seat across from his wife, that she was going to have to excuse herself so they could have a quickie.

Bonnie clearly read his intentions, for her face flushed. "Work now, play later."

Griff laughed, not at all embarrassed by Bonnie's diversion. He opened his laptop.

Bonnie said to Tally, "Get ready to start writing, then we'll split up the calls. Maybe between the two of us, we'll find someone who's seen him."

Tally pulled a pad and pen out of her purse, ready to go. She cast a curious glance at Griff, wondering what he would be doing.

As if he'd read her mind, Griff looked up. "I'm going to see if I can track his purchases."

Tally's eyes widened. "You mean…like hacking into his bank account."

"Kind of. Don't worry. I have a private investigator's license. It's all above-board."

"Thank God," Tally said, feigning relief. "I'd hate for us to find him, only to have him be forced to come visit us in a jail cell."

Griff grinned at her silliness.

Tally took the first half of the list and Bonnie took the bottom half.

One after another, they check-marked the name of the person with whom they'd made contact. With each negative response, both women grew more frustrated.

"How many do you have left?" Bonnie asked.

Tally counted. "Five. How about you?"

"Six."

They both glanced at Griff.

"Any luck?" Bonnie asked him.

"Not so far. The last two purchases I can find were on Tuesday. One at Pizza Palace and one at the pharmacy. Before that, he filled up his truck earlier that morning at the Chevron."

"We ate lunch at Pizza Palace on Tuesday. We ran into Lily, Sylvie, and Jani. They were having a Christmas shopping day and Lily's sister-in-law, Kat, and her husband, Todd, had the kids at PlayLand."

Bonnie shot her a look of concern. "Was it hard talking to Jani?"

"No, but I could tell she felt really bad that Jim's drinking-and-driving caused me injuries that left me in a coma."

"Poor thing. She feels really guilty about what he did."

"It wasn't her fault. She didn't force him to drink, or cheat on her, or to drive when he was stinkin' drunk," Griff said.

"But that's the kind of woman Jani is," Bonnie said. "She was technically still married to Jim, so she accepts responsibility for his actions."

"As far as I'm concerned," Tally said, "Jim is responsible for what he did, not Jani."

Bonnie glanced at Griff. "What was the pharmacy purchase?"

"That, my love, is none of our business."

Bonnie shot a look at Tally, whose face blossomed red. Bonnie grinned. "I get it."

Tally looked down a the last five names on her list—Coop Dawson, Murph O'Donnell, Spenser Pope, Ricky Almeida, and Ryker Manning. "This would have been a lot easier, if Sam had said who the friend was in his note." She scanned the list. "I recognize all the names except Ricky Almeida. Who's he?"

"They were all in Micah's class. Ricky and Sam were a couple of rabble-rousers back in high school and joined the U.S. Air Force the day after college graduation. They took some tests and were both allowed to enlist with Special Ops as their specialty of choice. Sam served four years, then came home and applied to the fire department, where he's been ever since. Ricky stayed in for ten years, got another degree after his service was up, then came back here last year."

"Funny, I don't remember him or Sam. What's his degree in?"

"They were a few years older than you, so that's not surprising. Sam got his degree in Engineering. Ricky's second degree was in Criminal Justice. He works for Griff now."

Tally had no recollection of her conversations with Sam pre-crash, and post-crash, they'd spent most of their time making love, not talking. She had no idea he'd led such an interesting life up to now. "Maybe Griff should contact Ricky."

"I could," Griff said, looking up from his laptop, "and I will. Check him off your list."

Tally nodded and dialed the next number. And the one after that, and that, and that. By the time she reached Ryker Manning's name, she was ready to give up. "Ryker is Zoë's cousin, right?" she asked Bonnie, her brain still a little fuzzy on some things.

"No, they're brother and sister, and he's a great guy, although I usually only see him at the Christmas Valley Inn when he's officiating at a wedding. The ranch keeps him pretty busy."

"Did he do your wedding?" Tally asked.

"He did and it was beautiful. Of course, the inn looked amazing, as it always does at Christmas." She slid a glance at her husband, who was frowning at the laptop screen, then looked back at Tally. "Sam told me he asked you to marry him."

"He did." Tally said nothing more as she relived him asking. *Will you marry me, Tally?* He'd kept it simple and straightforward and she'd answered in kind with, *Absolutely. Name the date.* "I thought he was having some fun at my expense."

"No way! He was dead serious," Bonnie said.

"Considering the number of people who've told me that Sam mentioned we're getting married, I no longer think his proposal was made in jest."

"Good, because Sam would never joke around about something so serious," Bonnie said.

"This is weird," Griff said.

"What, love?" Bonnie asked. She managed to stand and rubbed her belly as she walked around to his side of the table.

"I'm not quite sure yet. Let me do some further digging." He looked up at Bonnie with a smile, which morphed into an expression of concern. "You look tired."

"I am a bit, but I promise, I'll go straight to bed after we finish."

"I'm so sorry," Tally said with distress. "I'm being selfish when you've been on your feet all day at the Cottage. I can finish my calls at home."

"That might be best," Griff agreed, taking in Bonnie's swollen ankles. "In fact, if you're going in to work tomorrow, Tally. I think I'll keep my lovely wife at home until the baby comes." He put his big hand on her swollen belly. "She thinks she's Wonder Woman."

"That's because she is," Tally said. "I'll report in at eight, so I can re-acclimate myself."

"That's too early," Bonnie protested. "Quarter to ten is perfectly fine, and I'm sure it'll all come back to you right away. I'll text Zoë to give you a hand if you have any questions. She's been an absolute love, helping me out when I need it."

Tally nodded her agreement. "Thanks, both of you, for all your help."

"After I get Bonnie tucked in, I'll call Ricky, then keep looking," Griff promised, "and if you need help tomorrow, call me. I'm pretty good at ringing up sales, wrapping items, and carrying them out to the ladies' cars."

"He's being modest," Bonnie said with a wry smile. "When Griff's in the Cottage, the ladies come in droves to drool over him."

That made her husband blush, but otherwise, he took her comment with good humor.

Tally hugged Bonnie goodbye, then the girls, who could barely take their eyes off the TV, and finally Griff, at the front door.

"Just so you know, Bonnie's been having what the OB says are Braxton-Hicks contractions, which means she's really close, probably closer than the week she told you earlier."

"I remember Sylvie talking about those when she was pregnant with Logan, but I thought they occurred earlier in the third trimester."

"That's the thing," Griff said. "Bonnie had them about a month ago at irregular intervals, but today, she's been having them with more regularity."

Tally's eyes widened. "Have you been timing them?"

"No, but I'm thinking I should. Our little bundle of joy may be here sooner than we thought."

"Do you have someone to watch the girls?"

He nodded. "Granny and G'ma are going to take them, and Kenzie Manning will help out, if needed."

"Sounds like you have everything covered."

"Let's hope so." He glanced in the direction of the kitchen then back at her. "Just so you know, I'm trying to track Sam's phone via GPS."

"You can really do that?"

"Maybe. Let me know if you learn anything."

"I will, and thanks again for your help."

Tally made her way down the walkway, thinking about Ryker Manning. For some reason, she experienced an urgent need to talk to him.

She decided to take a chance and do it face-to-face.

Chapter 17

Tally took the back way to the Manning ranch via County Road 12. It was more scenic, though since it was after dark, she wondered what she thought she could possibly see.

She debated backtracking to the more well-traveled Valley Road, but the snow had stopped, which helped her make up her mind. CR12 it was.

Twenty-five minutes later, she turned onto the drive, which lead to Ryker's place. The Bar IM shingle, dangling from two iron chains, swayed lightly in the breeze.

Tally hoped she wasn't calling too late. Ranchers were known to turn in early, but it wasn't yet eight o'clock, so she felt fairly certain Ryker would still be up.

She knocked and he opened the door immediately, probably because sound carried up here in the middle of nowhere. At least he didn't have a shotgun pointed at her when he answered her knock.

"Tally," he said. "Sam told me you were out of the coma. Come in before you freeze your behind off."

"Thanks."

He closed the door quickly against the cold and helped her out of her coat. "I take it you're not with Sam."

"No, but that's why I'm here." She unwrapped her scarf and handed that over, as well.

Ryker hung her gear up on a horseshoe coat rack, frowning.

"What's wrong?" she asked.

"I'm not sure, but you being here is making me second-guess my decision yesterday not to call Sam after...." He trailed off, shaking his head.

"After what?"

"After I texted him about the reindeer."

"Reindeer?"

He nodded. "The Kringles are at the tail-end of renovating their barn. The reindeer were moved over to my ranch until the renovation is finished. They have the run of the meadow, but I noticed that one of them took off." He blew out a disgusted breath. "There's a pack of wolves hanging around and I'm worried they're stalking the reindeer. I texted Sam that I could use some help rounding up the one that wandered away, if he was free." He frowned again. "I never heard back from him, and that's not like Sam."

"When did you send the text?"

"Tuesday night, or rather Wednesday morning, around three a.m."

Being a firefighter, Sam would have heard his phone ping for a text message, even if Tally had slept through it. At that instant, her own phone rang. She pulled it from her purse. Griff Conte was calling, so she answered.

"Tally, I'm looking at my phone right now. Ryker sent me and Sam a text around three a.m. Wednesday morning, but for some reason, my responding text came back as un-deliverable."

"I'm at Ryker's now," Tally said, putting the phone on speaker. She glanced at the rancher and said, "Griff says he got your text, but his response never went through."

Ryker's brow furrowed. "Did Sam respond?"

Griff said, "I don't see anything, but that doesn't mean he didn't send one."

Ryker pulled out his phone and accessed his text messages. "I'm still not showing a response from him."

"Since I know mine didn't go through, maybe Sam's didn't, either."

"That is freaking weird."

"Since I moved here to the valley," Griff said, "I've noticed it's not uncommon for calls and texts to get dropped."

Ryker frowned. "True enough."

"Let's think about this for a minute. Tally never heard Sam get up, so we can probably safely assume that he disappeared sometime after three on Wednesday morning."

Ryker's gaze shot up to meet hers. "You were at Sam's place?"

Somewhat chagrined to admit it to a man who was an ordained minister on top of being a rancher, she nodded. "When I woke up, he was gone and I haven't seen or heard from him since."

"He didn't leave you a note?"

She nodded, then for Griff's benefit, said, "Yes, but it was vague." She pulled the note from the pocket of her jeans and handed it to him.

"He doesn't say where he was going or what it was about."

"I noticed that when Tally showed me the note," Griff said, "but where else would he be going?"

"Which way did you come on the drive out here?" Ryker asked Tally.

"CR12."

"Did you see anything out of the ordinary?"

"No, but then I wasn't looking at anything except the road."

Ryker jammed a hand through his hair, leaving it spiky. "I came up on Valley Road, which runs past the Christmas Valley Inn. I didn't notice anything, either, but like you, I wasn't looking."

Tally's insides churned with dread. "Something's happened to him."

"We don't know that yet," Griff cautioned, probably in

hopes of quelling her fears.

"Regardless, there's not much we can do about it to-night," Ryker said, "but tomorrow, when it gets light, I can take the helo up and look things over."

"We can't just do nothing," Tally said, agitated.

"We don't have a choice until morning, Tally." Ryker put a hand on her upper arm, as if to steady her. "We'll find him, okay?"

"Promise?" she asked, barely above a whisper.

"Promise," he said, his tone firm and confident.

Griff concurred. "I'll be out there to help you look, unless Bonnie goes into labor before then."

"Stay with your wife," Ryker advised. "From what you told me, she's ready to have that baby. You shouldn't be gallivanting around the countryside looking for Sam. I'll give Micah a call."

Tally wanted to volunteer to go up in the helicopter with him, but she'd already promised Bonnie she'd work at Gingerbread Cottage, and a promise was a promise. "You'll keep me updated?" she asked Ryker.

"Absolutely."

"You, too, Griff?"

"Count on it."

Tally drove home going the long way. Her emotions, in an uproar before she left Ryker's ranch house, had settled down. Whereas she'd bordered on freaking out then, she'd settled down to a manageable fevered pitch that was more like determination coupled with hope.

It didn't help when she walked into her apartment that the Christmas clock started up again with a song she was beginning to hate. This time, it sat on the mantle above her gas fireplace.

Was it her imagination, or was it dancing from side to side, showing off its idiotic ability?

An errant thought wiggled into her brain.

Or was it trying to make a point?

Tally thought sleep would be impossible, but nonetheless, she set her alarm for seven a.m., just in case. As it turned out, she was so exhausted, sleep claimed her almost immediately.

Her nocturnal wanderings took her back-and-forth, from dreams so hot she was writhing and moaning from the heat of them, to nightmares of Sam's ragged and torn body burning in the flames of hell.

When her alarm went off at seven, she was already awake and in the shower. She dried quickly, shut off the clock radio, and dressed. Anxious to be on her way, every task seemed to take forever until she finally pulled on her coat.

What stopped her was the Christmas clock, sitting on the floor in front of the door leading to the garage. Even as she watched, the hands spun round-and-round and the evil "Jingle Bell Rock" began to play.

Tally picked up the clock, watching in amazement as both hands landed on the twelve.

"This is just *too* weird. What are you trying to tell me?"

The music stopped immediately, without her having to push in the button on the back.

Bemused by the clock's antics (if a clock could actually have antics), she set it on the counter and made her way out to her new Fiat. She no sooner backed out of the driveway than the clock she'd just left on the kitchen counter appeared in the seat next to her. Instead of "Jingle Bell Rock," it played "The Twelve Days of Christmas."

Tally would have rather listened to the Seventies on Seven on satellite radio, but surprisingly, the version of perhaps the longest Christmas song ever, was palatable coming from the Christmas clock.

She let the clock play on, though she had laid it on the floorboard, in case she had to hit her brakes. She didn't want it to go flying and break. There would be no returning it to After Thoughts again, if that happened. With that settled, she pointed her car north to catch CR12.

It occurred to her as she reached the intersection for the turnoff to County Road 12 that the clock really might be sending her a message. With her foot pressed gently against the brake, she put on her left-turn signal and spared a glance at the clock. The hands spun and spun and landed again on the twelve.

Tally checked her rear-view mirror. No one behind her.

The music stopped.

She made her turn.

Normally, the speed limit was 50 mph, but on the snow-packed road, she was doing twenty miles an hour less. She had plenty of time to get to Ryker's place, even at a slower pace.

Five minutes later, the clock surprised her with yet another tune, "Grandma Got Run Over by a Reindeer."

"Are you trying to tell me that Sam's been run over by a reindeer?" she demanded with impatience.

The clock jumped right into "A Marshmallow World," a song she recognized because it was on her Dean Martin Christmas CD. The fact that she knew that shocked her. If she hated Christmas, why would she have a Dean Martin Christmas CD?

She sang along in her head until the song got to *get out and roll it along*.

"Get out?" she asked the clock.

The stanza repeated. Three times.

Tally checked her rear-view mirror again. She was alone on CR12. She passed milepost eleven and looked for a safe place to pull over. She didn't find it for a mile, where the road widened at MP 12 for a viewpoint observation. She signaled, eased off the roadway, put on her emergency flashers, and exited the vehicle. To keep the interior warm inside, she left the motor running.

Without knowing why, she scooped up a handful of snow and formed a snowball, though she didn't roll it along. Instead, she walked over to the metal guardrail and stared out at the vista before her.

The day had started out cloudy, but the overcast skies were beginning to break up, though the sun hadn't yet peeked through.

Tally tossed the snowball back-and-forth between her gloved hands.

The Christmas clock suddenly appeared in the snow at her feet, belting out "Blue Christmas."

As if being bombarded with an epiphany, realization dawned. The clock was trying to tell her where Sam was.

County Road *12*.

Milepost *12*.

Twelve days of Christmas.

Get out and roll it along.

Blue Christmas.

Aside from the nonexistent blue light bulb over her head, what was blue? The sky was full of dark clouds. The conifers were green and snow-covered.

She leaned over the guardrail, careful not to lose her balance as she peered downward. There it was, a blue ribbon of water. That in itself was puzzling, because the day was so gray, the river should have reflected the grayness, not a brilliant blue.

Tally glanced again at the clock. It broke into "Do You Hear What I Hear?"

Over and over, it stopped on the second line, asking if she saw what it saw. She dropped the snowball so she had two hands free and leaned further over the rail, firmly grasping the metal.

The clock switched to "Rudolph, the Red-Nosed Reindeer."

She inched out a bit more.

And there it was. Sam's *red* truck, over the side of the sheer wall of the cliff.

She fell back, lost her balance, and landed on her rear end. Her mouth formed a startled O. Why hadn't she noticed right off the bat that the guardrail was severely damaged?

Tally scrambled to her feet and leaned over the rail again, screaming as loud as she could, *"Sam!"*

Chapter 18

Sam jerked awake in the truck. Had someone called his name?

He listened, but didn't hear anything over the sound of the river rushing by, not more than ten feet from the truck.

Outside the cab, snow drifted down in big flakes, again. Great. If this kept up, not only would it be a white Christmas, but Mother Nature was evidently intent on giving them a white pre-Christmas, too, and at this rate, maybe even a white Easter.

He considered going back to sleep for a while, maybe get back into that dream where he and Tally were....

Not a good idea, he decided. He needed to take a leak, then eat something.

Sam climbed out of the truck and pulled off his gloves. Damn, it was freezing cold on top of everything else. He took care of business, hoping his wiener didn't turn into a Popsicle while it was exposed. He finished quickly and climbed back into the cab, using a bit of hand sanitizer before he pulled his gloves back on and fished out the other half of the Baby Ruth from the glove box.

He ate slowly. The constant ache in his head had wiped

out his appetite, but when he got out of this predicament, he knew it would come back. His plan was to head straight to Petey's Steak House for a big, juicy porterhouse, medium rare.

Even as he had the thought, the truck rattled to a stop. He knew he couldn't have exhausted the fuel supply trying to keep warm. Did that mean the gas tank *did* have a slow-leak puncture?

He turned off the ignition and pulled his phone out of the console. He'd attempted to get a signal a dozen times already with no success. He gave it another try, not that it mattered. The phone was dead and he had no way to charge it, because his truck was dead, too.

He swallowed the last bite of candy bar, examining the sky. It wasn't like he was in Antarctica, for Pete's sake. He was no more than twenty minutes from town, as the crow flies, and even less from Ryker's ranch.

His gaze wandered upward. He didn't have a snowball's chance in hell of making it up that cliff, but for the first time, he started to think about crossing the river to find another way out of the mess he'd gotten himself into. At the bend in the river, the current was swift, and it would be colder than a witch's tit, but he was fit, so he should be able to make it. There was a bridge further upstream, but he was having a hard time remembering it if was before or after the turnoff to Ryker's ranch. Either way, it would get him over to CR 12, giving him a better chance at survival.

If only his head didn't hurt like a bastard, he might be able to come up with rational plans.

He put his head back against the headrest and closed his eyes.

The tune, "I'll Be Home For Christmas," began to play in the cab. His eyes slitted open and he turned his head toward the sound. Tally's Christmas clock sat in the driver's seat, facing him. The hands spun and spun on the face, finally landing on the twelve.

Sam closed his eyes, thinking he was injured worse

than he'd originally thought.

In the next instant, he was deeply asleep.

If she'd arrived five minutes later, Tally never would have spotted Sam's truck because of the heavy snowfall. She yelled until she was hoarse, and still no answering response came back. She didn't like to think what that meant, but from what she'd seen earlier, her mind couldn't help tracking in that direction.

Please, God, don't let him be dead. Please, please, please.

She pulled out her phone, hoping for a cell tower out this way. Nothing. Not even a smidgen of a reception bar.

Did she go back to town, or drive on to Ryker's? Without too much thought, the ranch won, since she still had plenty of time before she had to be at work.

Ryker had a helicopter. If anyone could get to Sam, it would be the former Army Ranger. According to her brother, Ryker had served in Afghanistan and had experience flying Black Hawks on rescue missions. Micah had told her Ryker had filled in on several occasions when a pilot had been injured or killed, extracting his guys from life-threatening situations.

Somehow, some way, Ryker could bring Sam up from the floor of the canyon, or fish him out of the wild river roaring by his crumpled red truck, if that's where he was.

Tally jumped back into her new Fiat and steered onto the roadway. She drove toward the Bar IM Ranch, driving faster than the snowy road condition warranted.

She didn't care. Time was of the essence. She didn't have a second to waste.

Ten minutes later, she braked to a stop midway in the circular drive in front of Ryker's home. She dashed up the porch steps and banged on the door, screaming, *"Ryker!"*

The door flew open and there stood her brother. She hadn't even noticed his truck parked further along the drive. "Holy shit, Tally! What's going on?" Micah demanded.

"Sam!" she cried. "I found his truck."

"What the hell?" Ryker asked, coming up behind Micah. "Where?"

"You know that one long curve on CR12, at the viewpoint? He went over right there."

"Went over?" Ryker asked. He and Micah exchanged a look. "Are you sure? That's a straight drop down and it's snowing. How could you even see anything?"

Tally gave a brief thought to smacking her brother's old friend for questioning her, but said instead, "I leaned over as far as I could and I saw it. A red truck really stands out in the snow, Ryker. I'm not making this up." She glared at him for good measure. "Can you still take the helo up if it's snowing?"

Ryker glanced out the open door. "It's let up some, so I should be okay."

"You mean *we'll* be okay," Micah corrected.

"No, I mean me. I'm not taking up any passengers when we've got weather."

Her brother glared at him.

Tally said, "Ryker's right. Besides, you've got a wife and child at home, and another one on the way. If the chopper went down, it would be hell on your family." Left unsaid were the words *if you died.*

"I can't just sit here like a lump," Micah said.

"You won't be. Get on the horn and notify CVFD and the Mountain Search-and-Rescue team." He glanced at Tally. "*Exactly* where is he?"

"Milepost twelve, *exactly.*"

Ryker nodded and reached for his coat and hat. "I'll do a swing-by and get a feel for how we're going to get him out of there."

"Should I call the sheriff's office?" Micah asked. "They've got a boat."

"Might not be a bad idea. Let each agency know which ones you're talking to. They may have others to bring in, as well, and I'm sure they have contacts for equipment we might need."

Tally grabbed his arm. "Are you going to be able to get him out?"

Ryker glanced at her. "One way or another, I will."

Tally read between the lines. Ryker meant *dead or alive*, but being a kind man, he was apparently trying to spare her an emotional breakdown. "You can do it, if anyone can."

He smiled and gave her a quick hug. "It's good to have you back, Tally."

She nodded, but she wasn't so sure he was right. When a person was in a coma, they weren't cognizant of pain, either physically or emotionally. Right now, she was not only scared shitless, she was also hurting like crazy.

The last thing she wanted was to lose the man she was pretty sure she loved.

Micah pulled out his phone before the door closed behind Ryker. He called the fire department first.

While he was on the phone with CVFD, Tally called Mountain Search-and-Rescue. Another of her brother's friends, Asher Hammell, ran the operation. He answered on the first ring. Tally filled him in on the situation.

Ash said, "I'll get my team assembled and we should be there within the hour. Milepost twelve, right?"

"Yes. Thanks, Ash."

"Don't worry, Tally. You came back, and we'll get Sam back, too."

He said it with such confidence, Tally couldn't help but believe him. Outside, the helicopter began its warm-up.

Next, because Micah was still on the phone with CVFD, she called the sheriff's office and spoke with Veronica London, Sheriff John Pulkinen's receptionist and one of Tally's former classmates. Tally quickly explained about Sam. "Micah said you have a boat and maybe that would come in handy in the rescue attempt."

"I'll talk to the sheriff right now and get things rolling," said Veronica.

"Thanks, Ronny." Tally hung up and opened the front door. Ryker lifted off and his helo shot toward the west.

Micah joined her on the porch. "I wish Ryker had texted me to help find the stupid reindeer."

"Maybe he didn't because he knows Sylvie is pregnant."

"So is Bonnie."

"True, so why *did* he text Griff?"

Her brother made a soft grunting noise. "Griff's been helping out on the ranch. He likes horses and he likes the ranching lifestyle."

"How does Bonnie feel about that?"

Micah glanced down at her and shrugged. "She's ready to buy a ranch."

Of course, she was. Bonnie was a woman ready to take on new challenges. Which reminded Tally that she had to be at work by ten. She glanced at her watch. Nine o'clock. Forty minutes before she needed to head to Gingerbread Cottage.

"Close the door," Micah said. "We'll be able to hear when he comes back."

"I hope the snow stops soon."

Her brother studied the sky. "Ryker was right. It's letting up already."

"God, I hope so. I want everyone to make it through this day alive."

Chapter 19

Tally glanced at her watch every five minutes.

"Will you quit doing that?" Micah groused. "He'll be back before you know it."

"I have to work, remember? I want to know what's going on before I leave."

"I already told you, I'll call and let you know what's happening."

Tally nodded, but she wasn't appeased. "Micah?"

"Yeah?"

"What if he's...I mean, what if he didn't...."

Micah put his arms around her and gave her a hug. "Tally, honey, don't let your mind go there."

"When I came out of the coma and he was there in the kitchen with you and Mom and Dad, it really rubbed me the wrong way. I didn't recognize him. I didn't even know we had a history, brief though it was."

Micah drew back, amused, if his expression was anything to go by. "You made a quick turnaround on that."

"Yeah, well, I realized soon enough that I was attracted to him."

"I hope so, since you spent the night with him."

"It wasn't a one-night stand."

"I never thought it was."

"Do you think ill of me because I slept with him so quickly."

Micah barked out a laugh. "I'd be the last one to criticize you for doing something like that."

"Because of the way you fell for Sylvie?"

He nodded. "And the way Sylvie fell for me." He blew out a sigh. "All I can say is, sometimes you find yourself drawn to another person and you can't do anything but give into the attraction, sexually and otherwise."

"I can't believe we're having this conversation."

He grinned. "Neither can I."

The stared in silence out the big window in the living room.

"Do you love him?"

"God help me, I think so."

"He's going to make a great brother-in-law."

"No one said anything about marriage."

"Sam did."

Of course, he had. Had he told the entire town?

The sound of the helicopter's rotors could be heard in the distance. They both grabbed their coats and scarves and tore out the front door. From the porch, they watched as Ryker landed on the pad down near the barn. Once the rotors had stopped, they ran through the snow to greet him.

"What's the situation?" Micah asked.

"It's his truck, all right."

"Did you see any sign of him?" Tally asked.

"I didn't see him sprawled on the rocks, and I don't think he's in the river, or at least not at the crash site. He must still be in the truck."

"That's a good sign, right?"

Ryker nodded, though his grim expression said otherwise.

"Tally, it's almost twenty to ten," Micah said. "You need to get going."

She was torn. She really wanted to go back to MP 12

and keep tabs on what was happening. "You guys promise you'll let me know what's going on, right?"

"Promise," her brother said.

Ryker nodded his agreement.

With a great deal of reluctance, Tally climbed back into her Fiat. She'd made a promise and she had to keep it. Micah and Ryker weren't liars, either one of them. If they said they'd keep her informed, they would.

To keep her sanity, she had to rely on that.

Tally arrived at work with six minutes to spare before the store had to open. To her amazement, she remembered the opening drill.

When she unlocked the doors at ten, eight customers poured in from the FruityCakes bake shop, which was now called Yummies, and another five came in through the front door.

Zoë Manning stuck her head through the doorway and said, "Let me know if you need help. Stevie said she'll take care of Yummies, if I have to come over here."

"Thanks, Zoë."

The phone rang at eleven o'clock.

"Just wanted to let you know," Griff said, "we're at the hospital. More later." And with that, he hung up.

Zoë popped in to make sure Tally was doing okay.

"Hold the fort for a minute, okay?"

Zoë nodded.

Tally made a quick run over to the kitchen.

"What's up?" Charley asked.

"Griff just called. They're at the hospital."

"I knew she was close," Charley said. "I can hardly wait to see what pops out. I'll let Stevie know." She raised her hand and crossed her fingers. "Here's hoping it's a quick delivery."

"So many babies," Zoë murmured when Tally returned to the Cottage. "I feel like I need to find me a man and help add to the population."

Tally grinned, and not for the first time, wondered if she and Sam had started a new little life inside her before he'd begun using protection.

At noon, Zoë came to help out, since Kenzie was now manning Yummies. The phone rang again shortly after that. When Tally recognized her brother's voice, she signaled Zoë to take the register.

"We're getting ready to go down. Just wanted you to know you might not hear from me for a while."

"Are there a lot of people there?"

"A ton. Sam is well-liked in this community. Call Sylvie for me, will you?"

"Sure." And then the line went dead. Tally immediately called Sylvie. "Micah asked me to give you a ring. They're just going down for Sam. He said it could be a while before we hear anything."

"I hope Sam's okay."

"Me, too."

An uneasy silence seemed to scream from the phone. Finally, Sylvie said, "We have to think positive."

"I know, it's just that…." *Just that* what? Dammit, why couldn't she get her feelings and memories under control.

"He loves you," Sylvie said, as if reading her thoughts.

Tally hesitated. "Would it be really weird if I said I think I love him, too?"

"Don't ask me. Since I fell almost instantly in love with Micah, I might not be the right person to ask."

"I think that makes you *exactly* the right person to ask."

"Well, then, I say no, it's not weird, and I'd love to be your matron of honor."

The wedding again. "Did he take out an ad in the local paper?"

"Not quite, but he did tell us you said yes when he proposed."

Tally sighed. "I guess I did, but honestly, I thought he was joking."

"Then the question is, were you joking in response, or

did you mean it when you said yes?"

"I better figure it out, huh?"

"Absolutely, and not that I'm an expert, or anything, but you two are perfectly suited for each other."

"How do you know that?"

"I don't know, I just do." Then, "Logan, you can't ride Nugget, sweetie. You'll hurt his back." Nugget was Micah's golden retriever.

"You should buy that kid a horse," Tally said, only half joking. "While we're on the subject of dogs, how's Buttercup?"

"Didn't Micah tell you?"

"Tell me what?"

"Buttercup and Nugget are in the family way."

"I guess my brother thought I couldn't handle the news."

"That sounds like Micah," Sylvie said, her tone dry.

"I'll talk to you later."

Obviously distracted by her toddler and Nugget, Sylvie said, "'Bye," and disconnected.

At one o'clock, Griff called to say Rafael Conte had arrived. He weighed in at eight pounds even and he was twenty inches long. "He's beautiful, like his mom and sisters," Griff said with awe.

"Congratulations," Tally said. "I'll spread the word here and I'll be up to see Bonnie and the baby sometime this evening."

"She'll like that," Griff said. "Gotta go. They're going to let me hold him."

Two o'clock, three o'clock, and four o'clock came and went. The store was busy, which helped keep Tally's mind off what was going on at milepost 12 on CR12.

At five-thirty, she turned out the lights and ventured into the FruityCakes kitchen, where Stevie and Charley were sitting at a small table near the doorway, enjoying a hot chocolate.

"Any news about Sam?" Charley asked.

Tally pulled on her coat. "None. I'm going to drive out that way and see what's going on."

"Maybe you should wait to hear from Ryker or Micah," Stevie said.

Tally fastened her buttons. "Would you, if it was Spense over the edge of that drop-off?"

Stevie frowned. "No."

Charley nodded. "Me, either, if it was Tate, but be careful, okay?"

"I'll be fine."

"You're just days past coming out of a coma that lasted almost a year," Charley reminded her. "You probably shouldn't even be at work, let alone driving CR Twelve when it's snowing."

There weren't any windows in the kitchen and she hadn't looked out the shop window recently. "It's snowing again?" she asked with dismay.

Stevie nodded. "Has been for a while. What if I have Spense drive you up there?"

"I think he and Tate might have already headed that way," Charley said. She pulled out her phone. "Where are you? … No, everything's fine, I just thought you and Spense might be up on CR Twelve where Sam went over. … Okay, I'll keep dinner and other things warm for you." Her suggestive tone left no room for interpretation. "Love you, too." She disconnected. "They're at Ryker's ranch, searching for the reindeer."

"Reindeer?" Stevie asked with a laugh.

"Ryker is boarding Kringle's herd while they finish the rehab on their barn," Tally said. "One of them apparently got loose somehow." She shook her head. "I don't have a clue how a person goes about rounding up a missing reindeer."

Charley and Stevie shared an amused glance.

"I don't think Tate does, either," Charlie said, "but bless his heart for jumping in to try."

"I'm sure Spense doesn't," Stevie said, "but I gotta give that man credit. He's willing to learn how to do anything."

Tally wrapped her scarf around her neck and pulled her gloves from her pockets. "I'll check in later with you guys, if that makes you feel better."

They nodded.

"Don't forget," Charley said.

Tally waved and left via the back door of the kitchen.

She was surprised when she reached her vehicle. At least two inches of fresh powder had accumulated on the hood.

The snow couldn't have made Sam's rescue any easier for anyone involved, especially the man flying the helicopter.

Chapter 20

Tally reached the turnoff for CR12, only to discover that the road had been barricaded and a detour sign set up directing traffic to continue on Valley Road. She felt a little silly for not anticipating that. Out of necessity, emergency personnel would have closed the road. It was a narrow two-laner and their vehicles probably took up every inch of roadway the closer they got to MP 12.

She hopped out of her Fiat to move one of the barricades, drove through, then got back out and replaced it.

Between the snow and the snowpacked road, it took her nearly thirty minutes to reach milepost 12. There, she encountered a beehive of activity, and a scowling deputy sheriff. She parked well away from the yellow tape strung across the road.

Still, the deputy approached. His stride indicated he was stuffed full of grim determination. "This road's closed, ma'am," he advised her when she climbed out of her Fiat.

"I know," Tally said. "The thing is, that's my boyfriend down there."

The officer squinted at her, as if suspicious of her claim. "You're Tally Barrow."

"That's right."

"I thought I recognized you. I responded to the crash you were involved in last December." He shook his head. "I didn't know you'd come out of the coma, but glad to see you did."

"Thank you. It just happened this past week."

He held out his hand. "Mike Aaronson."

Tally accepted his gloved handshake. "Nice to meet you." She glanced toward the turnout. "Can you tell me if they've brought Sam up yet?"

"They haven't, but they're working on it."

Dismayed by the lack of information those few words imparted, Tally wondered who she could ask to speak to that might be willing to say more than that. From somewhere deep in her memory, she pulled up the name Avery Haversham. If she recalled correctly, he was the fire chief, and she'd met him over a year ago on the day she'd done the Christmas tree consult and decorating at the fire station. "Is Chief Haversham here?"

The deputy nodded.

"Do you think I could speak to him?"

"Sorry, but he's down below."

She wracked her brain for more names.

"Tell you what," Deputy Aaronson said before she could think of any, "if you promise to stay out of everyone's way, I'll let you come under the tape."

Tally flashed him a brilliant smile. "I promise I won't get in the way."

"Promise you won't fall over the side of that cliff, either."

"I won't. I mean, I promise, I won't fall over."

He lifted the yellow tape and she ducked under. "I hope your guy comes out of this okay."

Even though she was worried, she refused to consider any bad outcomes to Sam's situation. "He will."

On the small strip of snowy river bank, between the

cliff and Sam's truck, six men continued to discuss the best way to get Sam back up the sheer drop to the roadway.

Tired of waiting for them to figure things out, Sam intervened from where he leaned against the driver's-side door of his truck. "Look, guys, I know I'm not on the small side, but I have climbed before and I'm sure I can make it up once I'm harnessed."

Asher Hammell of Mountain Search-and-Rescue gave him a look. "You do know it's snowing buckets, not to mention it's dark as sin already."

Sam gave him a look right back. "I'm fully aware, Ash, and you forgot to mention, it's windy as hell."

"This would be a lot easier if the crane hadn't gone tits-up," Chief Avery Haversham said.

"Tell us something we don't already know," Ash said, scowling.

"Look," Ryker said, "we know we're not going to walk away from here and leave Sam on his own for another night, and none of us wants to spend fourteen hours out here waiting for daylight, right?"

The others murmured their agreement.

The chief planted his hands on his hips, which was no small feat because of his fire coat, and stared up at the cliff. Every other gaze followed his.

As cliffs went, this one wasn't anywhere near the height of the walls of the Grand Canyon, but it was still more than a hundred feet from the riverbank to the guardrail up above. They also had another problem—the sheer wall wasn't simply straight up-and-down. It sucked in at the bottom, as though God had tightened a wide belt around it, and there was ragged outcropping midway that posed an entirely different problem.

Rock Dennison, one of Ash's search-and-rescue team members spoke up. "Look, we decided at the beginning that it would be best to transport Sam up-top via the crane, but that option is gone. We have plenty of manpower, so we could pull him up by hand, but the problem with that is, he'd have to be an active participant."

Mack Kearny, the other guy on Ash's team, said, "That would definitely work if Sam was in tiptop shape."

All eyes turned to stare at the temporary sling cradling Sam's left arm.

"He'd need two hands and both feet to keep the basket away from the rocky face," the chief said.

"I can do it," Sam insisted.

Ash grunted. "It's not like this wall is made out of sponges, Sam. It's solid granite and ragged as hell. With this wind, you'd be beat to crap before you ever reached the outcrop."

Sam aimed a scowl at Ash. Friend or no friend, he didn't like to be told he couldn't do something, even if he knew ahead of time that he didn't have the strength to make the trip up the wall in a freaking harness. If only he hadn't stumbled on the rocks and injured his wrist and his knee. Had he stayed put when he heard the helicopter approach, he wouldn't be incapacitated right now. Given his occupation, he felt like a damned idiot

Ryker said, "If we transport him across the river, I can get him out of here in the helo, no sweat."

No sooner had the words left his mouth than the wind picked up and the lazy snowfall morphed into a fullfledged blizzard.

"You're crazy, Ryker," Ash said.

"If you'll recall, I've flown in worse."

Everyone there knew he'd flown a Black Hawk more times than he could count on two hands, and that he'd done it in adverse weather conditions and under fire. The good news was, he'd lived to tell about it, which stood in his favor.

"You're in a bit of a canyon here," Chief Haversham reminded him.

"Still doable," Ryker insisted.

Sam believed him, but apparently no on else did.

Literally and figuratively, he was stuck between a damned rock and a hard place.

Deputy Aaronson swore under his breath, then said to Tally. "Hold on a minute, Miss Barrow. Someone else is pulling up."

Impatient to move closer to the action, Tally nonetheless came to a stop.

"What's going on?" a woman asked.

Tally recognized the voice immediately and swung around. "What on earth are you doing out here, Jani?"

"I come up here a lot since…." She trailed off, leaving *the accident* unspoken. "Well, you know."

Deputy Aaronson apparently didn't accept that Tally and Jani knew each other. "Since I don't know, ma'am," he said, "why don't you spell it out for me?"

Tally couldn't bear the thought of making Jani respond. "Jani's husband is the one who hit my car."

As realization dawned for the deputy, he turned to Jani. "Sorry, ma'am. I didn't know."

Jani shrugged, as if the incident were nothing, when in reality, Tally knew it was everything. "What *is* going on?" Her gloved hand swept through the air. "I didn't know the road was closed. Is it an avalanche or something?"

Instead of filling Jani in, Tally asked, "Deputy, can Jani come under the tape if she stays with me?"

Aaronson's indecision lasted only a few seconds, but it seemed to go on forever. "Since she already came through the first barrier, I guess it'll be okay, but if you two cause any trouble, out you go."

Tally flashed him a smile. "Thanks."

Jani joined her a moment later. "What happened?"

"Sam went off the road at the turnout."

"Oh, no! Is he okay?"

"I don't know yet, but I'm hoping to find out soon."

By the time they reached the turnout, all the men were huddled near the damaged guardrail. Tally decided not to interrupt whatever conversation they were having via walkie-talkie with the men below.

"Isn't this a desolate spot to come out to on a cold winter night?" Tally asked.

Jani looked away, then back at Tally. "I guess it fits my mood these days." She sighed. "Jim and I used to love Christmas. We decorated and baked and sang Christmas songs together, and then everything changed."

"Because he found a girlfriend?"

"No, she came later. Things changed when I pushed him for a child."

Tally started. "You're kidding."

"I wish I was. We'd never really discussed having kids, but when we took care of Macey for Lily, he'd play with her, like she was his own kid. It never occurred to me he didn't actually want a child of his own, or that he'd react like he did." She sighed. "Honestly, I couldn't comprehend the radical change in him after that."

"I'm sorry to hear that," Tally said. "Did he ever say why?"

"Only that he didn't want kids, period."

"Wow, he must have been really good at hiding his true self."

"If you're trying to make me feel better, you're failing miserably."

Tally bit her bottom lip. "That came out wrong. What I meant was, maybe Jim didn't know he had an evil-twin side."

"You mean to the extent that he went out and found a girlfriend who loved to drink?"

Tally found herself at a loss for words.

"And after that, he drove drunk and ran into an innocent bystander and put her into a coma for almost a year?"

Something in Jani's tone alerted her to a troubling thought. "You're not thinking that I hold any ill will toward you, are you?"

"It may have crossed my mind," Jani admitted after a few moments. She looked away, her expression one of agony.

Tally hugged her. "Jani, the only person I blame for the crash is Jim, and as far as I can tell, you were an innocent bystander, too."

"Yeah, right," Jani said, holding on to Tally for dear life. "I drove him to cheating and alcohol, didn't I? How innocent could that be?"

Tally wanted to reassure Jani, but nothing she thought of to say seemed right. She wasn't, after all, a psychologist. What if she said the wrong thing?

Still, it didn't feel right to say nothing. She pulled back and gazed straight into Jani's tortured eyes. "Listen to me, okay? You didn't drive him to cheat *or* to drink. He was a grown man, capable of making bad decisions all on his own. The fact that he went to the dark side has nothing to do with you and everything to do with the kind of man he was."

Jani's teary eyes overflowed. "I wish…."

"Don't wish. You've got a new life now. You're smart, beautiful, and energetic. Forge a new path for yourself."

Jani swiped at her cheeks with gloved fingertips. "Is that what you're doing, after being in a coma for so long?"

"As a matter of fact, I think I am," Tally said. "Maybe we can help each other out."

"I'm willing to give it a go," Jani said, her tone halting. "At this point, what do I have to lose?"

Tally smiled. "Exactly. We're both young and the world is our oyster."

"Your pearl is Sam," Jani said, her voice tinged with sadness. "I don't have a pearl."

"But you will. This is Christmas Valley, remember? Good things come to those who wait, to utter a phrase my mother loves to death."

Jani laughed. "I love your mom."

Deputy Aaronson approached. "I thought you wanted answers."

"I do," Tally said. She glanced at the group of men clustered at the guardrail. They'd broken up.

"Tally!" her brother Micah called. "What the hell are you doing here?"

"I had to know what's going on," she told him.

He glanced curiously at Jani. "How're you doing?"

Jani managed a smile. "Surprisingly, I feel a little better after talking to Tally."

Tally smiled at her, but said to her brother, "What's the status?"

"The crane broke down, so we're trying to figure out how to get Sam up the side of that granite wall."

"What's the holdup?"

"The wall's not straight up-and-down. If we give it some manpower, we could pull him up, but we'd need him to have both hands and both feet free to navigate the irregularities, and he can't do that because he's injured."

Determined to focus on his injuries later, Tally frowned and concentrated on the rescue. "What's the alternative?"

"Ryker's going to bring him out in the helo."

"In this weather?" Huge snowflakes fell so thickly, visibility was worsening by the minute.

"Ryker's flown in worse."

"That's no assurance of success," Jani said, "and just because Ryker moonlights as a minister doesn't mean he's exempt from something bad happening."

"I'm with Jani on this," Tally said. "Can't you get in another crane?"

"We tried. This rescue calls for a specific type and there's only one of them here in the valley. The company that runs it requested a repair crew, but they can't be here for two days." Micah planted his hands on his hips and looked toward the drop-off with a worried expression. "We can't wait that long."

"What about putting a boat on the river and taking it down to the next boat landing?" Tally suggested.

"This isn't that kind of river," Micah said. "Look, it's freezing-ass cold out here. Both of you should go home and get warm."

"I don't—"

"No arguments, Tally," her brother cut in. "The two of you aren't doing anyone any good standing around here. Go. Home."

Home was the last place Tally wanted to be, but she knew Micah was right. "Want to go somewhere close to the hospital and get some dinner?" she asked Jani.

"Sure, why not?" Jani glanced toward the overlook.

"Good," Micah said, and turned to go back to the guardrail.

Jani said, "Maybe they'll let you speak to Sam before we go."

Tally wondered why she hadn't thought of that. She called out to her brother, "Micah, will they let me say hello to him?"

"I'll check with the firefighters. They're the ones who have the walkies." He came back a minute later. "Sorry, Tally, they've already started across the river."

Disappointed, but hopeful, Tally said, "Promise you'll call me the minute they set down."

"It might not be at the hospital," Micah warned her.

"Where else would it be?"

"Since the weather's bad, it could be anywhere."

Tally didn't waste time with more questions her brother wouldn't have the answers to.

Instead, she began to pray for Ryker and Sam's safety.

Chapter 21

Tally and Jani met at Spanky's Poor Boy. Not only did Spanky's serve the best burgers in the valley, but it was close to the hospital.

Tally glanced out the big window next to their table. The snow had gradually subsided, thank goodness, but no helicopters had landed.

The two of them were dawdling over hot chocolate when Tally's phone rang. Micah. She grabbed it and swiped the ACCEPT button. "It's about time you called."

"Hello to you, too," he said.

"What's happening? I thought I'd hear from you an hour ago."

"I'm at the hospital."

"Has he been admitted?"

"No, he's not here yet. Ryker landed at his ranch, since it was closer. They had an ambulance waiting, and it should be here shortly."

The ER ambulance bay was directly in Tally's line of vision. She'd have a perfect view when the transport carrying Sam arrived.

"Where are you?" her brother asked.

"Jani and I are at Spanky's. Should I stay here or head

over to the hospital now?"

"Wait until you see the ambulance pull in. No sense hanging out in the lobby, if you don't have to."

"Want me to bring you something to eat?"

After a brief pause, Micah said, "That would be great."

"You want a bacon cheeseburger?"

"Yeah, with fries. Order it in triplicate."

"You must be hungry."

"Ash is here with me and Ryker is following the ambulance in."

The muffled wail of a siren sounded in the distance.

"I hear it coming in. See you in a bit." Tally relayed to Jani what little information her brother had to offer, signaling the server as she spoke. She gave her order and asked that it be wrapped so it would still be hot when she walked across the street.

"Want me to come with you?" Jani asked.

"Only if you want to."

"Maybe I can be your support team, since you'll be surrounded by mountains of testosterone."

Jani's tone was so wry, Tally couldn't help grinning.

The ambulance pulled in under the portico and unloaded its precious cargo. Ryker's truck was close behind. On this snowy evening, he had no trouble finding a parking space.

Ten minutes later, Tally and Jani walked into the nearly deserted ER waiting room. Micah, Ash, and Ryker stood near the coffee pot, drinking coffee.

"Have you heard anything yet?" Tally asked, handing over the large handle bag to her brother.

"Not yet," Ryker said, tossing his paper cup into the trash. "They're just getting started. He was conscious when we put him in the helo, but fell asleep as soon as we got in the air. He woke up long enough to be put on the gurney, which he bitched about profusely, then promptly fell asleep again before they had him loaded into the ambulance."

"Men aren't very good patients," Jani commented.

Ryker peeled back the wrapper on his burger. "Says a woman," he responded with good nature. "Thanks for the food, Tally."

"Yeah, thanks," Micah and Ash said in unison.

"You're welcome. Should we sit down? I mean won't it be easier to eat if you sit?"

The three former military men laughed.

Micah said, "Tally, honey, I can eat standing on my head, and I'm pretty sure Ash and Ryker can, too."

Five minutes later, Grey Dixon stepped through the double doors that separated the waiting room from the treatment area.

Tally frowned, knowing Dr. Dixon was a neurologist. Before she could ask if he was treating Sam, her brother spoke up.

"Hey, Grey. Did that bump on his hard head do any damage?"

Grey grinned. "Not that I can tell, but he does have a concussion."

"He has a bump?" Tally asked, though they ignored her.

Grey went on. "He also has a broken wrist and a sprained knee. To be on the safe side, they'll stick him in all the machines and run all the tests, to make sure there's no other broken bones or any internal injuries." Grey made eye contact with each of the men. "I hear he went off CR12 at the overlook. He's damned lucky to be alive."

Tally asked, "Did they call you in specifically, or where you already here?"

"I hung around after Micah called to tell me what was going on." He tilted his head at her. "What are you doing out in this weather?"

Tally didn't feel like going into a long explanation about her day. Instead, she gave the neurologist an extremely modified version. "Jani and I had dinner at Spanky's." She took a breath. "When can I see him?"

"Funny you should ask. He wanted to know when he could see you, too." Grey grinned again and shook his head. "Lovebirds."

Tally favored him with a frown, which made the doctor laugh.

"I told Sam I'd check to see if you were here, and if you were, I promised to bring you back." He shifted on his feet and crossed his arms over his chest. "He doesn't need to be riled up, though. Can you handle seeing him bruised and battered without creating a fuss?"

"As long as he's alive, I can handle anything."

He studied her for a long moment, then nodded.

Tally found herself confused about why Sam thought to ask if she was in the waiting room. "How'd he know I'd be here?"

Ash spoke up. "Micah mentioned you were up-top, when we were walkie-talking, trying to figure out how to get him out of the predicament he'd got himself into."

"He was none too happy about being carted across the river," Ryker said, "especially when he got disoriented and capsized the raft."

"You're not wet," Jani said, her tone slightly accusatory.

Ryker didn't seem to mind. "Since I landed at the ranch, I changed after they got him into the ambulance."

"You're not wet, either," Jani said, looking at Ash with what Tally could only define as suspicion.

"That's because I climbed back up the wall. Helos are Ryker's thing, not mine." He shook his head. "My momma drilled more sense into my head than Ryker's got in his."

Ryker grinned. "You're FOS, as usual. That snow was nothing more than a little blizzard."

Ash, Micah, and Grey laughed.

Tally was glad the three friends could find a moment of humor in the rescue, but she didn't find the situation funny at all. She needed to see Sam in person, so she'd know for sure that he was okay.

She also needed to look him straight in the eye, which was the only way to know if he was serious about marrying her. Crazy as it seemed, she needed that reassurance to help her figure out if the feelings she had for him were real. She didn't mean feelings in a temporary crush kind of way. She meant feelings that leaned toward love. Feelings that might already *be* love. Feelings that would last a lifetime.

It never occurred to her that the frantic worry eating at her meant she already knew the answer.

Grey took Tally back to the treatment area.

She'd been there only once before, but she had no recollection of it. The silence bouncing off the walls kind of threw her. "Are there other people here?" she whispered.

Grey glanced down at her. "Not many. They tend to stay home and not do things that would require a visit to the ER when the weather is bad."

"Was it quiet like this when they brought me here?"

"No. For one thing, it was morning and though it was cold, the roads weren't like they are now." He flashed her a look that she interpreted as sympathy.

"I always thought drunk drivers usually hit other vehicles after dark."

"Yeah, well, that's a popular misconception. Ask any ER in the country, and they'll tell you, drivers under the influence of booze or drugs send them business all day long." He stopped in front of a treatment room. "Here we are." He glanced at his watch. "I'll give you ten minutes alone, then he's off for an MRI."

Tally checked her own watch. Though she hadn't known Grey Dixon long, she knew he meant business and expected his mandate to be followed. "Ten minutes it is. Thank you."

"Go easy on him."

Surprised, she asked, "Why would you think otherwise?"

He shrugged. "To tell you the truth, I have no idea why those four words popped out of my mouth."

"Hunh. And you're a neurologist."

He smirked. "That's what they tell me." He stood aside so Tally could enter the room, then pulled the door shut.

Chapter 22

Sam lay on the bed with his eyes closed. His even
breathing indicated he might be asleep.

Tally glanced at the monitor beside his bed. His
blood pressure was elevated and his pulse was a little faster than normal, but his oxygen level was good. "Sam?"
she whispered.

No response.

She tiptoed over to the side of the bed, debating whether or not it would be okay to touch him. The urge was so
strong, the part of her that needed the physical connection,
to be convinced the electronic equipment wasn't lying,
won the argument. She placed a hand on his forearm.

His eyes came open at the contact. "Tally."

"Hi, Sam."

"God, it's good to see you."

"It's good to see you, too. When I looked over that
guardrail and saw your truck, I was afraid you were...."
She couldn't utter the *dead* word.

He lifted his right arm, the one with the blood pressure
cuff attached, and laid his hand against her cheek, caressing it. "I'm too stubborn to die when I have a wedding in
my future."

Tally leaned closer. "Is it okay to kiss you?"

"I'll die, if you don't."

She expected his lips to taste different. They didn't. She expected the kiss to be chaste. It wasn't. She feared she might feel nothing. Instead, she felt everything.

"Climb up here and lie next to me, Tally."

"But—"

"No buts, just do it. I need to feel you against me."

Tally dropped her purse on the floor and wriggled out of her coat, then figured out how to lower the bedrail. She climbed up, certain she was going to catch hell from the ER staff.

"That's better," he said, wrapping his right arm around her. "You kept me alive, Tally."

"I did?"

He seared her with his intense dark eyes. "When I wasn't trying to figure out a way to climb up that granite wall, all I could think about was you."

She opened her mouth to speak, but he shushed her with a slight shake of his head.

"You probably think it's all about the great sex, and I'll grant you, I've never experienced anything like what we shared, but it's more than that. We had three days together before the crash, and a couple of days together since then. I'm in love with all of you—your brain, your heart, your humor, your ditziness."

"Hey, I'm not ditzy!"

He smirked. "If you say so, but I still love that side of you. I also love your tenacity and your determination and your kindness to others. Shall I go on?"

She readjusted herself to prop up on one elbow. "Maybe later," she breathed against his lips. "For now, though, I'd like you to kiss me again, and don't stop until my ten minutes are up."

"Ten minutes?"

"Grey's timing my visit, then you go for an MRI."

"We'd better make the most if it, then. Can I cop a feel?"

"I'd be disappointed if you didn't." She readjusted herself to make it easier for him.

"This is probably the first time you've been groped by a guy with a blood pressure cuff on one arm and a sling on the other." He worked his hand under her sweater and up to her breast. "God, this must be Heaven instead of the ER."

She savored the feel of his fingers against her nipple as she sought his lips again. His erection pressed into her belly.

"I really need to get naked with you."

"Ditto."

"If they don't let me go home tonight, I want you in my room and in my bed, and if they don't like it, they can sign my release papers."

Tally wriggled in his arms, which resulted in him groaning, though not with pleasure. She stilled, then pulled away. "What did I hurt?"

"It's my wrist."

She broke away from him in a crazy, fumbling maneuver and hopped out of the bed. Shaky with remorse for having caved in to his request to climb into bed with him, she rearranged her sweater before she raised the bedrail again.

"*You* didn't hurt me, love. I forgot and grabbed you wrong."

"I completely spaced that Grey said your wrist is broken."

"With you in my arms, I did, too."

She glanced at the arm sporting the sling. "I'm so sorry, Sam. I wasn't thinking. I never should have...." She trailed off and swung her hand over the bed.

"Hey, don't sweat it. I liked what was going on, too, you know."

She reached for her coat and slipped it on. "That doesn't excuse me climbing up into the bed with you."

"Tally—"

"I have to go, but I need to ask you a question. Were

you serious when you asked me to marry you?"

His expression faltered. "Of course, and you said yes." He frowned. "You did say yes, didn't you?"

"I thought you were kidding."

"I don't kid about serious stuff like marriage." His frown deepened. "Have you changed your mind?"

Frustrated, Tally didn't know how to respond. She'd mistakenly thought when she heard his answer, she'd have hers, too. "This is all so quick, Sam."

"I've had a year to think about it," he reminded her.

"That's the problem, isn't it? I've only had a week to think about it."

He looked away, probably hoping she wouldn't see that she'd hurt him, but he was too late. It was obvious that her words had cut deeply.

"I'm sorry, Sam."

"So am I, Tally. I hope I haven't caused you any embarrassment."

"I'm not embarrassed. I liked what we were just doing. I liked it a lot."

"I'm talking about embarrassing you with regard to a wedding that's not going to happen."

The door pushed open and Grey walked in, followed by a no-nonsense-looking nurse who gave Tally a reproachful glance.

The opportunity to finish her conversation with Sam was gone.

Tally buttoned her coat. When was she going to learn to think before she spoke? She directed her gaze to the neurologist, who had a stern look on his handsome face, as if he knew exactly what had just happened.

"You okay, Sam?" Grey asked his friend.

"Sure," Sam said, his tone dull.

The doctor turned to Tally. "Your ten minutes are up, Tally. Do you remember the way back to the lobby?"

She nodded, her eyes again on Sam. "I'll wait."

"You don't need to," he said, unable to meet her gaze.

"I want to."

He looked at her then, his expression blank.

Tally realized she really needed to finish the conversation she'd started with him. Maybe she still had a chance to redeem herself with the man she thought she loved.

The hallway seemed much longer on the way back to the waiting room.

Jani, Micah, Ryker, and Ash sat in a corner, talking softly.

Tally walked right on past to the ladies room. Once inside, she made sure the other stalls were unoccupied. Only then did she let her tears fall.

She was an idiot, there was no doubt of that. She'd hurt Sam and he hadn't been able to hide it from her. That, in itself, told her volumes about him.

He wasn't a guy who was afraid to show his emotions, even if those emotions were killing him, but she was pretty sure he didn't realize how much he'd revealed to her.

She'd been looking for a sign, and there was every chance that sign had just slapped her in the face. The problem was, she still wasn't sure. Did she love Sam, or not? Could a person know something like that in just a few days?

One thing she did know was that she hadn't meant to hurt him. He hadn't done anything mean or nasty to her. He was a kind man. A loving man. That was evident from the way he'd made love to her.

Sam wasn't the problem. *She* was.

Now, what was she going to do about it?

First things first, she splashed her face and patted it dry. This indecisiveness was pointless. No more tears. No more wallowing in self-pity because she didn't know which path her heart wanted to follow.

Sure, she could keep on having a sexual relationship with Sam, and it would be glorious, but it was obvious that Sam wasn't leaning that way. He wasn't the kind of man who would keep having sex with a woman just for the hell of it.

He was the kind of man who married a woman, made babies with her, and lived a long, happy life with her.

He'd get up in the middle of the night to feed and diaper those babies, and he'd make dinner when she didn't feel like it. He'd clean up afterward, too. And then he'd make passionate love to her all night long, if that's what she wanted.

He'd do all that for her, but what was she willing to do for him?

That's what stumped Tally. She'd never felt like this about a man before, so she wasn't sure *what* she'd do for him, aside from giving as good as she got, sexually.

This required some thinking. Alone. In her solitary bed. Without Sam to influence her thoughts.

But…she'd told him she'd wait, so wait she would.

Her eyes were red, but maybe no one would notice.

She pulled open the door and went back to the lobby. The men had their coats on and Jani was on her phone. "What's going on?"

"Grey just came out and told us we might as well go home," Ryker said. "In addition to the CT scan and MRI, Sam has to undergo some other tests. They're going to admit him overnight, to be on the safe side."

"I told him I'd wait," Tally said.

Jani disconnected her call. "Grey specifically said you were to go home." She avoided looking at the three men behind her. "I just spoke to Stevie, who said you're on the work schedule tomorrow. You should get some rest."

"C'mon," Ryker said, taking her arm. "I'll give you both a lift over to your cars. I noticed them parked at Spanky's when I drove in."

"But, I told Sam I'd wait," Tally said again.

"Honey," Micah said, his tone gentle, "from what Grey said, Sam doesn't want you waiting."

It felt like her brother had kicked her in the gut. Did everyone know she'd been awful to Sam? Her face flamed as she pulled on her gloves. "Thanks for the offer, Ryker, but I could use some fresh air."

To a person, they glanced at her with concern. Good grief, she couldn't even have a moment or two of self-chastisement without observation. She forced a smile. "I'll be fine. Really. My car is only a block away."

"I could walk with you," Jani said.

"I need some time alone," Tally said.

No one bothered to point out that she'd have plenty of time alone when she got home for the night.

Chapter 23

Tally took advantage of being at the hospital and made a detour to the maternity ward.

"I know it's getting late," she said to the nurse at the Obstetrics counter, "but I had to work today, then I went out to CR12 to see if they'd been able to bring Sam up yet, and now he's in the ER, and...."

She ran out of steam. It was no doubt TMI, but it was the way Tally did things.

"I heard Sam had gone off the road at the overlook on CR Twelve," the nurse said. "I'm glad to hear he's alive. How's he doing?"

"He's going through a battery of tests," Tally said.

"My husband works with him at the fire station."

"He does? Small world, huh?"

"Isn't it? Jeff will be glad to hear Sam's okay. All the firefighters are worried about him." She picked up her personal phone, then remembered why Tally was there. "Bonnie's in room three-twelve. Knock before you go in, and try not to stay too long."

"Thanks" —she glanced down at the nametag— "Didi."

"Jeff said Sam really changed when he met you last year. He was happy again. I'm really sorry about your accident and the coma."

"Thank you," Tally said. It seemed everyone in the valley knew about her and Sam, which added to her guilt over not being sure of her feelings for him.

She moved down the hall to room 312 and knocked, as instructed. A moment later, the door eased open. She shoved her gloves into her pocket and pumped the hand sanitizer dispenser.

Griff said, "Hi, Tally. Come on in. We were just wondering what happened to you." He gave her a hug, then stepped aside so she could enter the room.

Bonnie snuggled Rafael against her breast. "Hi, Tally. You just missed this little pig having his dinner."

"I take it he's a good eater."

Both Bonnie and Griff chuckled.

"He took to suckling like he'd had lessons before he popped out," Griff said.

"Like father, like son," Bonnie said in a dry tone.

Tally stepped closer to have a better look at their baby boy. "He's beautiful."

Bonnie smiled. "We think so."

"How are you feeling?"

"Like I could sleep the night through, but I'm sure Rafe has other ideas."

"Who has the girls?"

"They're at Joss and Lachlan's right now, but they'll go out to FruityCakes tomorrow." Her lips twitched. "As you can imagine, Granny and G'ma are looking forward to spoiling them."

Griff grinned. "Joss and Lach thought they could use some practice taking care of kids."

"I heard Joss is pregnant." Tally reached out a hand and caressed the baby's cheek with the back of her index finger. What she wouldn't give to make a baby with Sam.

The thought brought her up short, even though she'd considered it before. She pushed the possibility into a corner of her mind, to think about later.

"They're releasing me tomorrow," Bonnie said. She

glanced at Griff, then back at Tally. "How's Sam doing? We heard they brought him into the ER."

Tally pulled her hand back and did her best to fight off her tears. "He was headed for an MRI when I left."

Bonnie frowned. "Didn't you want to wait for him?"

"He didn't want me to."

"Honey," Griff said, "don't go getting in the middle of this."

Bonnie sighed. "You're right, it's just that…." She grabbed Tally's hand. "You and Sam are meant for each other. I hope you can work things out."

Tally blinked, trying to dissolve her tears. She forced a smile. "I guess if we're meant to be, it'll happen." With her emotions threatening to overcome her, she said, "On that note, I'm going to head home." She glanced again at baby Rafe and felt her heart clench. "Congratulations and let me know if I can do anything for you."

She hurried out of the room, but as the door closed, she heard Bonnie say to Griff, "I really need to have a talk with Sam."

Tally pulled into her assigned parking space and made her way up the walk to her apartment.

She wasn't the least bit surprised to hear the Christmas clock spewing "Winter Wonderland" when she walked through the door, even though she'd fully expected "Jingle Bell Rock." She hummed along as she pulled off her snow boots and hung up her scarf and coat.

When it got to the part where Parson Brown could marry off the happy couple off when he was in town, she let out a little scream and bolted for the kitchen.

Only the clock wasn't there. That's when she realized the music was coming from her bedroom. She charged down the hall, and there it was, in the middle of her bed. "You really know how to taunt a girl, don't you?"

The hands spun and landed on the big green 12.

"I got your first message, so why do you keep mocking me with the twelve? I know you don't have a brain, but I thought you were smarter than that."

In response, the stupid Christmas clock broke into "Baby, It's Cold Outside."

"Tell me something I don't already know!" she snapped and whirled away, headed for her closet. She stripped off her clothes and climbed into a pair of pink flannel pajamas adorned with black poodles and Eifel Towers. She left on her socks and shoved her feet into slippers.

She turned off the light and headed for the kitchen. The Christmas clock, which had beat her there, belted out yet another song to torment her, "Do You Hear What I Hear?"

Missing "Jingle Bell Rock" for some obscure reason, Tally grabbed a meat mallet from the utensil crock and approached the obnoxious clock. "I don't hear anything but you," she cried, "and I'm getting sick and tired of it!"

She raised her arm and took aim.

The clock disappeared, but its music played on. From the living room, "Dominic the Donkey" blared so loud, she was certain the neighbors could hear it. She threw down the mallet, and in an angry huff, made her way to the living room. "Okay, I get it. Every song you play has a message, and this time, you're telling me I made an ass of myself, right?"

The clock abruptly switched to "Joy to the World."

Tally rolled her eyes in disgust. "I don't appreciate your musical editorial comments!"

She threw herself on the sofa, staring at the clock on the steamer trunk. She tried to figure out the how-and-why of the clock, but came up blank, except for one thing. It had played "Jingle Bell Rock" constantly, until it got serious about giving her clues to Sam's whereabouts. Did that mean it was giving her clues to something else now? Was someone else in trouble?

As if it had read her mind, the clock hands began to spin, landing this time on the nine. The musical notes of "Holly, Jolly Christmas" filled the room.

Tally glanced at the mantle clock. Granny Marigold had left it to her mother, and her mother had given it to her as a housewarming gift when she moved into the apartment. It read 8:45.

Irritated, she realized she was toe-tapping to the music. She pulled her feet up under her. "What's so important about nine o'clock?"

Even as she voiced the question, the clock broke into "Run, Run, Rudolph."

Tally flew off the sofa and began to pace her small living room.

The clock had given her hints before, so it stood to reason, it was giving her hints again. All she had to do was figure out what those hints were, and what they meant. A wedding. It was cold out. She was supposed to hear something. Then she was being an ass, and after that, the clock screamed the equivalent of *hallelujah* because she recognized the stupid donkey clue. And now, it was all about holly and jolly, and before that, Rudolph was running. What the heck?

"Holly, Jolly Christmas" took over again.

How was she supposed to have a holly, jolly Christmas when she was drowning in misery?

Tally woke up curled under a blanket, on the floor, in front of the fireplace. She'd always been thankful that she had a gas fireplace, but falling asleep all night on the floor in front of it was not on her list of favorite things to do.

She stretched and groaned. Why hadn't she gone to bed to do her thinking? At least she would have wakened without aches and pains.

Her eyes sought the Christmas clock where she'd last seen it, on the steamer trunk, but it wasn't there. Thank heavens! Maybe it was gone for good.

Wondering what time it was, her glance wandered to the mantle. Granny Marigold's clock canoodled with the

Christmas clock. "Don't even think of making clock babies!" she snapped.

A moment later, she was on her feet. The time was five 'til nine. She had to be at work by nine forty-five. On this cold, snowy morning, did she have time for oatmeal?

The answer, she decided, was yes. She heated the milk-and-water, then added the oats, set the timer for five minutes, and hurried to her bedroom for quick shower and tooth-brushing.

The oven timer was reminder-dinging when she streaked naked to the kitchen to dish up her cereal. She added sugar, dried cherries, and a healthy dollop of half-and-half, then ran back to her bedroom to dress. The oatmeal had cooled sufficiently to eat by the time she returned.

Upon entering the kitchen, she discovered the resituated Christmas clock in the middle of her kitchen table. Great, company for breakfast.

"Christmas at Our House" began to play. Even though she was enjoying her oatmeal, Tally suddenly found herself hungry for oatmeal–raisin cookies. She was also overwhelmed with nostalgia for the years she'd helped her mom bake Christmas goodies.

Maybe she actually *did* love Christmas, which didn't explain why she'd woken from her coma thinking she hated the holiday.

It also didn't resolve the issue of the Christmas clock. Why did the hands now twirl wildly until they came to rest on the nine?

She cleaned up the kitchen, then called the hospital to see if Sam was still a patient.

"He is," said the woman who answered the phone, "but he as a DND posted next to his name."

"DND?"

"Do not disturb."

Crushed, Tally knew that was because of her. She thought fast. "Is there any chance you can connect me with Dr. Grey Dixon?"

"Sure, but since it's Saturday, it's possible you'll only get his voicemail."

How many times could a girl get kicked while she was down? Still, Tally was nothing if not polite. "Thank you."

Surprisingly, Grey answered a moment later.

"It's me," Tally said in her beaten-down voice.

"By me, I presume you mean Tally."

"Yes. How is he?"

"Do you really care?"

That stung, and here she'd thought him kind and considerate. "Of course, I care. Otherwise, I wouldn't have just tried to call his room."

"He has a DND on."

"So I discovered, which is why I called you."

His sigh carried over the phone line. "He's okay."

Okay? That was it? "That's a relief. I was afraid you'd find internal injuries when you did the other tests."

"Nope."

Tally'd had enough. "You're my doctor, too, right?"

"In a manner of speaking."

She'd hoped to goad him into being a little more forthcoming, but then she remembered that he and Sam were old friends. His loyalty obviously fell in only one direction. "Thank you." Fighting back tears, she disconnected the call without saying anything further.

If she wanted more comprehensive information about Sam, she was going to have to talk to the man himself. The problem was, she had to go to work. Any conversation she had with him would have to wait until after five-thirty.

Her mind whirled with possibilities as she left her apartment and drove to work. Gingerbread Cottage was hopping all day long, but because she was good at multi-tasking, she still managed to formulate a plan.

If all went well, she'd be sleeping in Sam's bed before the night was out, and even though he was injured and might not be able to engage in any lovemaking, there were things she could do that would let him know how she felt.

Afterward, they could snuggle together and discuss their future.

If only she'd known then how the remainder of her day would go, she might not have been so optimistic about how her night would turn out.

Chapter 24

At five-thirty, an exhausted Tally locked the front door, cashed out the register, and handed over the day's receipts to Stevie, who was the FruityCakes CFO.

"You're kidding me!" Stevie exclaimed.

Tally frowned, still feeling the ill effects of sleeping on the floor. "Darn, and I thought we had a pretty good day."

"Charley, come look at this!" Stevie called to her sister.

Charley hurried into the small office. Stevie stuck the printout from the Cottage cash register under her nose.

"OMG, is that for real?" Charley cried.

Stevie said, "This is a record-breaker, Tally. Did you cast some kind of spell over the customers?"

"No." Tally glanced at Charley, who had a big smile on her face. "I was hoping we had a good day, but I wasn't mentally tracking sales."

"It was an *incredible* day," Charley said. "Coupled with what we sold in Yummies, sales were terrific. If this keeps up, we're going to have our best year ever."

"I wonder if we've got enough merchandise to carry us through Christmas," Stevie said, frowning.

"We still have an order coming in, and Lily's on top of the cottage-industry stuff." Charley shrugged. "Would it be so bad if we ran out before Christmas and had a couple extra days to regroup before our day-after sale?"

"If there's nothing left," Tally said, "what would there be to sell the day after?"

"All the New Year's stuff, plus we learned pretty quickly last year that customers started shopping for Valentine's Day right after Christmas."

Tally blinked. "They did?"

The sisters nodded.

"What time does the store open tomorrow?" Tally asked. The evening she had planned with Sam was starting to look like a non-event. She was so wiped out, if she closed her eyes, she'd likely fall fast asleep.

"Oh, we're not open on Sundays yet," Charley said.

"I guess Bonnie forgot to mention that," Stevie added.

Charley shot her a sly grin. "That'll give you and Sam an entire day to yourselves."

Tally forced a smile, something she'd been doing too much of lately.

Stevie nodded. "Spense said Sam was really grumpy when he dropped him off at home, but I'm betting a dose of Tally will lift his spirits immensely."

"On that note," Tally said, hoping she sounded upbeat, "I'd better get going." So, Sam was home, was he? That required a new plan, but she wasn't discouraged. Him being at home again was better than him still being at the hospital, especially since she could do something tonight.

"Don't do anything we wouldn't do," Charlie said, laughing as she turned back toward the FruityCakes kitchen. As CBO, or Chief Baking Officer, no doubt she was looking forward to taking Sunday off, too, to spend time with her family, or knowing Charlie, baking with her family to ensure the FruityCakes went out on time.

Tally grabbed her stuff and left through the Yummies door. It was closed, too, but a group of ladies lingered over their coffee and FruityCakes while Kenzie wiped down tables and swept. Zoë helped by cashing out the register.

All was well in the world of FruityCakes.

Now, if only all could be well with her and Sam.

As she drove home, she concentrated on revamping the simple plan she'd originally concocted for the following evening. Surprisingly, a new one came to her without much effort.

If Sam was grumpy, it was probably because of her. He might not appreciate her showing up in the only sexy dress she owned—a little black number that exposed too much cleavage and too much leg. She'd bought it to wear for the dipstick who'd turned out to be married, only she'd never worn it.

But, a plan was a plan. Didn't her mother always say, you wouldn't succeed, if you didn't try?

As soon as she walked into her apartment, she stripped and got into the shower. Once out, she called La Tavola, one of Sam's favorite restaurants, and ordered dinner for two. "It's for Sam Reed," she said, "so you choose his favorites and I'm fine with anything."

"*Si, si*," Angelo said, "*e grazie!* What time, Tally?"

She glanced at the small clock on the shelf in her bathroom. Next to it, spinning its hands, was the Christmas clock. The hands landed on the nine. "Six forty-five?" As soon as she disconnected, it began to play "All I Want for Christmas Is You."

Tally towel-dried her hair then used the hot-air brush on it. She wasn't much on makeup, but this was a special occasion, so she applied some eye shadow, a little mascara, and a bit of lipstick. Along with the little black dress, she'd purchased a sexy black bra and skimpy black bikini panties, again, never worn. She also had black heels (never worn), which she decided to carry to Sam's front door and switch out with her snow boots.

At seven, she set down the bag carrying dinner on Sam's front porch and traded her snow boots for the three-inch heels, praying she wouldn't fall on her ass stepping inside his house. She'd practiced walking in them for ten minutes before she'd left her apartment and deemed herself ready to face the world.

She rang the doorbell three times and knocked twice, but no Sam. She automatically glanced at his driveway to look for tire tracks, then remembered his truck was over a short cliff and probably totaled.

Ready to give up and go home, she gave it one last shot. Nothing. She picked up the bag and her snow boots and turned to step off the landing.

The door flew open with Sam bellowing, "For God's sake, Grey, didn't I tell you to leave me alone?"

She swung back, teetering on her heels, and lost her balance. Trying to stay upright, the snow boots went flying one way and the dinner sack went the other. Tally flailed, overcompensated, and fell face-first into the snow bank beside the walkway.

For a moment, she couldn't move.

Seconds later, an arm curled around her middle and yanked her to her feet. "What the hell, Tally! What are you doing here?"

Sam plopped her down rather unceremoniously on the cleared landing, glaring at her.

Tally had a mouthful of snow, which she promptly spit out. Tears rolled down her cheeks. Hoping he couldn't tell the difference between tears and the snow coating her skin, she swiped them away.

"Speak up!"

"I brought you dinner."

"I'm not hungry." His glance landed on the La Tavola bag. "But I guess I could probably handle a bite or two."

Tally didn't know whether to run or face the dragon. A hopeful person might have detected a softening to his tone. A non-hopeful person would have turned and slunk back to her car in defeat. She decided to face the dragon, fire-breathing or not.

It wasn't like he was actually angry, but it was obvious he was still hurt, and she was the cause of it.

He reached for the bag and her snow boots, then his gaze slid to her feet, encased in the heels. His eyes trav-

eled further up her black-stockinged calves. There his pe-
rusal stopped, because she wore her long black wool coat.
Without another word, he turned and stomped back inside.

The optimist inside her took it as a good sign that he
hadn't slammed the door behind him.

She took several tentative steps forward, debating
whether or not he'd actually left the door open as an invitation to enter, or if he planned to come back and shut it in
her face.

Go in. You brought dinner for two, after all.

Tally took a deep breath, like that would give her some
courage, and stepped into the house. She closed the door
behind her and stood there like a lump, wondering what to
do next.

"If you're going to eat with me," he bellowed from the
kitchen, "you best not be showing up at my table with
your coat on."

She took her cue from that and slipped out of her coat,
which she hung in the guest closet with her scarf. Knowing her hair was probably as scraggly as it was damp from
the snow, she finger-combed it and made her way to the
kitchen.

Sam pulled plates and silverware from the cabinets one-
handed. "You can set the table."

Tally nodded, but didn't speak as he handed over the
dishes and utensils. It took her a moment to meet his gaze.
What she saw in his eyes made her gulp. Maybe he didn't
hate her, after all.

"Are you going on a date?" he asked, his voice rough
with accusation and some emotion she couldn't define.

"No."

She turned her attention to the table.

"Why are you dressed like that, then?"

"For you," she said, keeping her eyes on what she was
doing.

"You're difficult to keep up with, Tally."

"I'm sorry. I don't mean to be." It suddenly hit her that
her plan was idiotic. The last thing Sam wanted was to see

her. She shouldn't be there, practically groveling to be forgiven, virtually begging to be seduced, or if she were being honest, to seduce him.

If she had a brain in her head, she'd run out the front door and drive far, far away from here, and from Sam. That, and only that, would leave him free to find a woman who wasn't *ditzy*.

From the rustling sounds behind her, she knew he was unpacking the food Angelo had so carefully packaged in containers he'd promised would keep everything warm.

Hopeful coward that she was, she said, "I need to use the restroom," and hurried off without sparing a glance at him.

In the bathroom, she stared at her reflection in the mirror. Black streaks ran down from her eyes. That's what happened when you went face-first into the snow, then started crying. If only she owned waterproof mascara. She snatched a tissue from the box and made repairs, then stared eye-to-eye with her reflected self. "Now what?"

Shouldn't the answer come easily?

In this case, she decided that turning-tail and running off into the night would serve no purpose. She wasn't hungry for anything except Sam, but that wasn't gonna happen. She could sit at the dinner table with him and pretend to eat, then make up some excuse why she needed to leave. That would be the polite, if pitiful thing to do.

She'd stupidly thought she could mend things with the man she loved, but his harsh attitude spoke volumes.

There was nothing left to salvage between them, and it was all her fault.

Chapter 25

Sam pulled two tapers from the bottom drawer and slipped them into candleholders. Tally was offering him an apology, of sorts. Dinner, a nice bottle of wine, tiramisu for dessert. The least he could do was accept it, and her company, graciously.

God, he couldn't get the image of her out of his head.

A little black dress, revealing her beautiful cleavage. Sheer black stockings, showing off her beautiful legs. Three-inch heels, which she'd probably never worn before, judging by the way she wobbled in them. All for him.

He was humbled. Plus, he felt like a rat for the way he'd treated her in the ER, especially after Grey had pointed out that it was probably because she'd been unsure of herself and her feelings for him. He'd also reminded Sam that Tally had been in a coma for almost a year. She had a lot of catching up to do.

He lit the candles and shut off the main kitchen light. Before he could set the stereo to some soft, sexy music, Tally's Christmas clock appeared on the dining table. It was playing a slowed-down version of "All I Want for Christmas."

Sam experienced hope and melancholy all at once. It never occurred to him to wonder how the clock had appeared. After what had happened in the truck, nothing about the clock surprised him anymore.

He didn't hear Tally approach as he closed his eyes and wished for the one thing he might not ever be able to have, not this Christmas, or for any of his future Christmases.

Tally stood silently in the doorway, listening. What was that ridiculous clock doing here at Sam's?

Apparently determined to relay its musical message, the clock finished its rendition of "All I Want for Christmas" and switched to "Santa, Bring My Baby Back to Me."

A Golden Oldies aficionado, Tally recognized the Elvis song right away. The way he jerked at the change in tunes, she wondered if Sam did, too.

She moved into the kitchen and stood beside him. "The clock is magic."

His eyes flew open. "Magic," he repeated, his tone dubious, as if her elevator didn't go all the way to the top.

"Yes, it gives us musical messages and we have to interpret them."

It was obvious from the way his jaw clenched that Sam was battling some internal demon.

"I'm not kidding."

"I'm sure you *believe* what you're saying, but it's just a clock that plays music."

Even if his words hadn't relayed his thoughts, his tone was so skeptical, she almost caved in to the urge to keep her mouth shut. Almost, but not quite. That just wasn't her way. "After we took the clock back to After Thoughts, I was sure I'd never see it again, but when I got home, there it was." She sighed. "It was always one step ahead of me in my apartment. In the kitchen, in the bedroom, in the living room. It kept reappearing and playing 'Jingle Bell

Rock,' until I thought I'd go crazy. Then, it appeared in my car, still waxing musical. By that time, each song was different, but the hands still spun around and kept landing on twelve, and finally, I figured it out."

"You were having after-effects from the coma."

That stung. "Dr. Dixon said I wouldn't have any after-effects."

"You heard what you wanted to hear."

Had she? Were hallucinations possible after you'd been in a coma for nearly twelve months? Since she had no valid argument or confirmed facts to rebut him, she decided to plunge in all the way with what little evidence she had. "The hands always landed on twelve, which started me thinking that it was giving me a message."

Sam looked away, his expression troubled.

"I drove out to CR Twelve and pulled off at milepost twelve, which coincidentally happened to be the overlook." Something was bothering him, but she couldn't figure out what, unless he'd just realized he'd hooked up with a crazy cat lady who had no cats. When he didn't say anything, she asked, "What are you thinking?"

"Honestly, I don't know what to think."

"Just start talking. Maybe that will help."

Finally, he said, "The clock visited me."

That threw her. "After you went over the guardrail?"

"Yes." He shook his head, as if to clear it. "I thought I imagined it was there."

"You didn't." She looked up at him, her eyes wide with wonder. "If it hadn't been for the clock, I never would've gotten out to look over the side. It started playing 'Blue Christmas,' and the only thing I could see that was blue was the river. It was such a gray day, I knew the water couldn't be reflecting blue, but it was, and then the clock switched to 'Rudolph, the Red-Nosed Reindeer.' I leaned over even further and saw your *red* truck down there. I screamed your name, but you didn't answer." She sucked in a shuddery breath. "I've never been so scared in my life."

"Scared of what?"

"That you might be…dead."

"I went over the edge because I was trying to avoid hitting a reindeer in the road."

"What?" she said on a gasp.

"I guess the Rudolph song meant something."

Stunned, Tally said, "I guess it did."

His beautiful brown eyes churned with some emotion she couldn't identify.

She put a hand on his arm. "The clock helped me find you, Sam, and after that, it was all up to me."

His gaze skittered away. "You called for help."

"No, there's no cell service on that section of road, so I did the next best thing and went to Ryker's ranch. I kept thinking about his helicopter and how he'd flown rescue missions in the war."

He looked back at her. "After all was said and done, that helo was exactly how he got me out of there."

"The crane broke, so they had to do something different."

"That's what they said." His gaze dropped to her lips, then lifted to her eyes. "Thank you for being so persistent."

"It was the least I could do." She wanted to add, *for the man I love*, but something held her back. The old Sam might have already had her his arms, or even his bed, but the new Sam remained reserved, slightly aloof, and pretty much unemotional.

"Now what?" he asked, stepping away from her.

She sighed with resignation, feeling the futility of the situation deeply. "I'm trying to figure that out."

Chapter 26

Blowing out another sigh, Tally decided to keep talking about the clock, rather than probe her relationship with Sam. "The clocks stops on the nine now. I know it's giving me another message, but I haven't it figured out yet."

Sam tore his gaze away from hers and glanced at the table. One moment the clock was there, spinning its hands like crazy, landing on the nine, and the next moment, it vanished. "I don't get it. Magical Christmas clocks don't happen in real life."

"I don't get it, either. Maybe we're really in Wonderland and the White Rabbit will come hopping through at any moment, muttering, 'I'm late, I'm late!'"

A small smile lifted the lips she'd like nothing more than to kiss.

"Maybe we're both having hallucinations, or something." He shook his head. "Me from my concussion, you from the coma."

She couldn't dispute his assumption, especially since she'd had exactly the same thought.

"I distinctly remember that you returned the clock to After Thoughts."

She'd mentally gone over that territory herself, but she was willing to let him play the situation out in his own mind. "I did, and when I got home, there it was."

"This sounds like some kind of dark fairy tale."

"I thought so at first, but after it told me where to find you, I'd say it's more enlightened than dark."

He grunted.

"I've decided to keep it."

"That's a little creepy, don't you think?"

"Not really." She decided to inject a lighter note into a conversation that desperately needed levity. "You never know when I'll have to rescue you from another life-threatening situation." To her credit, she managed to deliver her words deadpan.

To Sam's credit, he laughed. He swung his head around and met her gaze, then lowered his eyes to take in the view offered by her neckline. "You sure you dressed up for me?"

"Absolutely positive."

"We should eat before everything gets cold." He pulled out a chair for her.

Tally sat. "I love the candlelight."

"I've never eaten with candles on my kitchen table before," he admitted. "I bought them on a whim one day about six months ago."

She smiled up at him and caught him admiring her cleavage again. "They're beautiful."

"Yes, they are."

She knew he wasn't talking about he candles.

He sucked in a breath when he looked up and caught her smile.

"Did Angelo include a good wine?"

"Beats me, but he's the expert, so I'm guessing it is." He poured a glass for her and one for himself before he took his seat. "This is quite a spread."

"I asked Angelo to make selections that you favored, so I'm glad everything meets with your approval."

When both their plates were full, Tally picked up her

wine glass and had a taste. "Nice."

Sam did the same and agreed.

"Tell me what happened."

Sam didn't act like he didn't know what she was talking about. "As I said, there was a reindeer in the middle of the roadway when I came around that last curve. I tapped my brakes and swerved, but I must have hit an icy patch, and the next thing I knew, I was over the side." He described what it was like going off the road and landing near the river, alive. "I honest-to-God couldn't believe I wasn't dead."

"Maybe your guardian angel was watching out for you."

"Maybe so, because I swear, it felt like the truck was cushioned when it hit the ground."

"Miracles happen every day," Tally said, thinking of her own coma.

"I suppose it *was* a miracle, because there's no way I should have survived that landing."

"I'm eternally grateful that you did, and that your injuries weren't debilitating." She hesitated. "They aren't, are they?"

"Aside from a broken wrist, a sore knee, and a bump on the head, which gave me a minor concussion, I'm in tip-top shape." He frowned. "I can't fight any fires until my wrist is out of the cast, but the chief says he'll still let me ride along and observe." A wry grin split his face. "Guess he knows I'll be a bear if I can't work."

Careful not to meet his gaze, she asked, "So, no other restrictions?"

"No. Guess I got lucky that way."

The longing in his voice brought her head up.

"I want us to be more than just friends, Tally."

She met his intense gaze across the table. She was pretty sure the emotions in her heart were reflected in her eyes. "I do, too."

"What are we going to do about it?"

"Finish dinner?" she suggested.

"And after that?"

"Clean up?"

"And then?"

"Go to bed?"

He let out a breath of relief. "Geez, for a minute, I thought you'd never get there."

Tally used her fork to fiddle with the pasta on her plate. "There's one other thing."

"What might that be?"

"We know we're dynamite in bed."

He smiled. "We sure are."

"But how do we know we'll be compatible in every other way?"

"When two people love each other, don't they take that leap of faith?"

"I don't know. I've never been in love before."

"Not even now?"

She set her fork down and reached for her wine glass, draining it.

"Geez, Tally, if you have to drink half a glass of wine to answer that question, you must be as far away as the moon from knowing the answer."

"I'm conflicted," she admitted.

"About what? Things seem pretty straightforward to me."

"That's because you've been in love before."

"No, it's because I know I'm in love with you."

"But what about your wife?"

Some deep emotion kept him from answering right away.

"It's okay. You don't have to talk about her."

"No, I think I need to."

Uneasy now for having brought up the subject, Tally squirmed in her chair.

"Missy and I dated in high school. We were your typical quarterback–head cheerleader couple. It seemed like the next logical step in our relationship was to get married, but our parents objected because they wanted us to go to college." He reached for the wine bottle and refilled her glass. "We both lived in the dorm first quarter, then decided it would be a cost savings if we got an apartment together." He made a wry face. "In reality, we were thinking of the sexual part of our relationship, not the financial end of it."

"When did you finally get married?"

"After we graduated, but before I shipped out. I served four years in the Air Force, and something happened while I was overseas. I was never sure if Missy found a boyfriend to fill in for me, or if she just fell out of love with me, but when she insisted she didn't want any kids and moved into the spare bedroom, I knew our marriage was over. We still spoke and made necessary decisions together, but we never slept together again."

"Why didn't you divorce her?"

"I took my marriage vows seriously."

Tally couldn't fault him for being honorable. "I'm sorry things ended up that way between you."

"Thanks. It was hard at first, but as the weeks passed, I guess I kind of got used to living with a roommate instead of a wife, and then she found out she had ovarian cancer." He shrugged. "In retrospect, I thought our relationship might have recovered if they'd caught the cancer early and she'd gotten treatment. Without the threat of a pregnancy hanging over her head, we might have been able to make things work."

She heard an unspoken *but* at the end of his statement. "What happened to make you think otherwise?"

"Her boyfriend showed up at the memorial service and introduced himself to me. He was pretty torn up about her death, saying they'd been trying to have a baby and that's how she discovered she had cancer."

"Oh, Sam, I'm so sorry."

He lifted a shoulder. "I took her death, and the fact that she no longer loved me, pretty hard for a while. I filled in on holidays for a lot of guys at work who had families. I sold the little house we lived in and bought this one. I thought it would erase the memories, but that only comes with time. I do love this house, though. The years passed and I matured enough that I no longer hold my self responsible for the failure our marriage."

"I'm sorry you blamed yourself at all for her actions."

"As I look back on our relationship now, I realize we were too comfortable in our stagnant relationship to see that we weren't suited for a life-long commitment."

She almost didn't pursue that, but she had to know. "And you think we are?"

"I know we are."

Tally hated that she still had doubts. "How can you be so sure, Sam?"

"Honestly, I don't know. I just am."

She took a long sip from her wine glass. "I wish…."

"What?"

"That I could understand. You were sure enough to marry Missy, and now you're sure enough to marry me."

"You've got it all wrong. I had doubts like crazy about Missy, but once we were married, I had to honor my vows."

"You had doubts?"

"Mega buckets full."

"So, why did you get married, then?"

"I almost didn't, but Missy begged me, and I'm a sucker for tears, so I did."

Knowing what she did about Sam, that made sense. She picked up her fork and took another bite of *pollo con parmigiano.*

They finished their meal in companionable silence and cleared the table together. "I'll take care of rinsing and putting the dishes in the dishwasher. Do you have something I can put the leftovers in?"

Sam pointed to a cupboard next to the refrigerator.

Tally put what was left of dinner into a container he could microwave, then turned to the sink.

"Do you want dessert now or in a while?"

"In a while is fine by me." She puffed up her cheeks. "I'm stuffed."

"I really like the looks of you from over here," he said, leaning against the opposite counter.

Tally wiggled her hips.

"Be still my heart."

She glanced at him over her shoulder, this time, wiggling her eyebrows at him.

He gave her a seductive grin.

The Christmas clock chimed in with "Baby, It's Cold Outside."

Tally closed the dishwasher door and wrung out the dishcloth.

Sam stood, arms folded over his chest, watching her.

The Christmas clock moved over to the counter.

The hands spun madly, then stopped on the nine.

Tally glanced at her watch. "I think I know what the clock is trying to say."

Sam lifted his wrist, before he remembered it was casted. His eyes shot to the clock on the microwave. Nine o'clock. His hungry gaze met Tally's. "Bedtime."

"Maybe," she said, advancing on him in a way she hoped was more than a little seductive. Standing toe-to-toe with him, she continued. "Or, it could mean it's time for me to head home."

"I don't think so."

"I don't think so, either."

He leaned down and took her lips.

Tally didn't wait to participate. She went up on her tip-toes and threw her arms around his neck, opening her mouth for him.

"Bedroom," he murmured, his breathing ragged.

"Stop talking and get me there.

Being a firefighter, Sam knew exactly how to pick her up without hurting his broken wrist and carried her down the hall.

Chapter 27

Sam set Tally down and leaned against the bedroom doorway, watching her walk toward his bed. No matter which way she turned, she was so damned sexy, even tottering in those silly heels. "I'm torn."

She stopped just short of his bed and turned, offering him a smile that curled his guts. "Don't worry, I'll be gentle."

"That's not what I'm torn about."

"Then what?" she asked, her smile faltering.

"I don't know whether to ravish you or take my time and savor every delicious inch of you."

"Can't you do both?"

"Not at the same time." He pushed away from the door frame and moved toward her. "I'm also torn about getting you out of that sexy little number you're wearing."

She tilted her head.

He stopped about two feet away from her and reached out a hand. His fingertips grazed her skin, following the scoop of her neckline. "Do I take off every damn thing you're wearing, or do I stand back and watch you do it?"

Tally visibly trembled. "Which idea are you favoring?"

He uttered a confused grunt. "Both."

"I'll start." She reached behind her and lowered the zipper on the dress that would have clung to her like a second skin if she hadn't been ten pounds lighter. "Now you." She gave him a come-hither smile. "We'll share."

Sam didn't need a second invite. He reached out to push the cap sleeves off her shoulders, cursing the cast on his left wrist. "I may be slow at this."

"Slow is fine with me. I'm not going anywhere."

It took him longer than it should have, considering his cast, but he couldn't resist touching her everywhere he could while he peeled the dress off her body. Once it pooled around her feet, she stepped out of it, almost falling over because of the heels. "Sweetheart, put your hand on my shoulder and kick off those ridiculous shoes."

"Thanks," Tally said. "My outfit needed them, but I never wear heels."

Several moments later, he stood and stared down at her. Her black bra was about as skimpy as it could get and still be called a bra, and boy, what it did for her breasts. His gaze traveled down to the bikini panties, caressing her curves as if they'd been made just for her. His fingers itched to sneak inside the front of those panties and make her come right there and then. He resisted the urge and let his gaze wander down to the black stockings, banded on the top with lace, which apparently held them up.

He inserted a finger beneath the lace and it stretched outward. Taking advantage of the little whimper she made as approval to continue, he managed to roll the stocking down one-handed and ease it off her foot. He repeated the process on the other leg.

Tally shivered and reached up to unfasten the front clasp of her bra. She shimmied and it fell to the floor, on top of her dress.

That left just her panties, but first, Sam couldn't resist tasting her breasts.

Tally's legs gave out on her when Sam put his mouth on her breast. She'd had big doubts about lovemaking with him again. How could it be even better than before?

He gave his attention to one breast, then the other, then pulled away and said, "You know what's next."

She nodded and slid her fingers into the tops of her black bikini panties. She wanted to rip them off, but for Sam's benefit, she made a spectacle of removing them. By the time they reached her ankles, he was breathing heavily, but more importantly, his desire was plainly evident behind his flannel sweats. "My turn."

He nodded, but didn't speak.

By then, Tally was in a hurry. She managed to get his sweatshirt pulled up to his chest, but he was so tall, she had to let him tug it over his head. She tackled his sweats next. Thanks to his boxer briefs, which showcased his erection well, she managed to get them down his long, muscular legs. He helped by stepping out of them, then kicked them aside.

Tally ran her hands up his legs as she stood, but hesitated when she landed at eye-level with his tented boxers. "I could make you really happy right now."

"Tally, you're already making me really happy, and I appreciate the offer, but save it for later, okay? Right now, I need to be inside you in the worst way."

Tally tugged the boxers down.

Sam was unprepared when she kissed his erection. "No fair," he said through clenched teeth.

Satisfied that she hadn't misjudged her action, Tally pressed herself against him as she pushed herself up.

"God, Tally…."

Tally couldn't think, all she could do was feel. She loved the feel of her breasts pressed against his erection, then his abdomen, and finally his chest. Sam was all man, and she couldn't wait any longer for what he'd promised.

She whirled away to pull back the bedcovers, then threw herself on the bed and opened her legs, inviting him in.

They made love for hours. Sam was remarkably adaptive when it came to his casted wrist. Tally discovered she could also work around the cast. She'd had no idea she could be so inventive.

At two a.m., they wandered naked into the kitchen to eat dessert.

"Let's sit in front of the fireplace," Sam suggested. "You grab the tiramisu and forks while I get a spot ready for us."

Intrigued, Tally complied. She also grabbed the wine bottle and two glasses, and put everything on a round pizza pan, since she couldn't find a tray.

In the living room, the fire crackled, because Sam actually had a wood fireplace. The light of the flames cast a romantic glow over the blanket and nest of pillows he'd spread in front of it.

"I could eat you alive," Tally said, studying his beautiful body from her higher vantage point.

He gave her a lazy smile and his gaze dropped to the spot between her legs. "I could eat you alive, too. After we finish the tiramisu."

Tally's legs turned to rubber. "I don't understand how a look or a word from you can turn me to mush."

He hopped up to relieve her of the loaded pizza pan. "You do the same to me, love, which is why I know we're meant to be together forever."

He leaned over and set the food and wine down, then straightened and slid his hand between her legs. His casted arm sought her breast while he laid one helluva hot kiss on her.

Tally moaned, wondering how it was possible that he could make her come so many times.

Sam held her tight, so she wouldn't fall.

When he'd finished, she asked, "Does it hurt your hand to play with my breast?"

"My hand is so excited by your beautiful boob, my wrist doesn't dare complain."

She grinned up at him. "You have such a poetic way with words."

"Let's eat," he said, pulling her down beside him, "then we'll eat again."

Tally could hardly wait. Every second with this man was a new adventure.

By Sunday afternoon, Tally was absolutely certain, she'd never be able to walk again. It wasn't just that Sam had incredible recuperative powers, either. She was flat-out satiated from sex, but then he'd rise to the occasion and she'd realize she could never have enough of him.

They ate dinner in front of the fireplace—cheese, crackers, salami, Mandarin oranges, and cold beer.

"I wonder," she began, but then lost her nerve to complete her thought.

"Wonder what?" he asked, feeding her a segment of orange.

"If I'm, you know…pregnant."

Sam's hand stilled at her lips. "We've been using condoms."

"But we didn't at the beginning."

"True." He thought about it for another moment. "I hope you are."

She stared at him with wide eyes. "You do?"

"Sure. That's what happens when a man and a woman fall in love and screw their brains out. They make babies."

"I'm surprised you feel that way."

"Why? I asked you to marry me, didn't I? You agreed, and even though you never mentioned protection, I thought it behooved me to take care of it." He frowned. "Are you already on some form of birth control?"

"No." She laid a hand against her belly. "Just so you know, I can't think of another man on Earth who I'd rather have be the father of my children."

He nestled his head against her abdomen. "So, you *are* going to marry me?"

She nodded, then realized he couldn't see the motion. "You bet I am."

"You ready for more dessert?"

"With you, I'm ready for anything."

At ten p.m. Tally rolled off of Sam. "You've spoiled me rotten."

"How so?"

"I'm going to expect this kind of sex for the duration of our marriage."

He chuckled. "I hear tell, by the time I hit 75, I may be a dud."

"That's okay," she said, feigning seriousness. "I hear tell that women reach their prime when they turn seventy, so you'll be able to get your jollies from pleasuring me."

He belted out a laugh at that. "Pleasuring you? Sweetheart, it will be my pleasure to pleasure you."

Content, Tally threw an arm over his chest and stroked his nipple. "I need to go home. I have to get up and go to work tomorrow, even if you don't."

"We haven't set a date yet."

"A date for our wedding?"

"Yes."

"Don't get mad, but I completely forgot we actually have to make plans for that."

"You have been busy with other things."

Her hand wandered lower and captured his hardening johnson. "That makes it your fault that a wedding date completely slipped my mind."

He closed his eyes and sucked in his breath when her lips traveled a path down to her hand. "Tally."

"Shut up, Sam, and let me give you a proper good night before I have to leave."

Chapter 28

Tally couldn't remember the last time she'd slept so well. She woke at eight, had breakfast, got dressed, and headed directly to Sam's house.

When he opened the door at 8:45, his bed-head gave away that he hadn't yet started his day. "Good morning, beautiful."

"'Morning, handsome. I thought maybe we could have a quickie before work."

His eyes flared and he pulled her inside and slammed the door, locking it.

Tally wriggled out of her shoes, coat, and slacks, then pulled her sweater over her head.

"No bra," Sam said, going for a breast.

"It's in my coat pocket. I thought it would save time."

"You have a great brain, Tally." He scooped her up and within seconds, they were in his bed.

At 9:40, Tally reluctantly left the tumbled mass of bedding and got dressed.

Sam watched her with hungry eyes. "What time does the shop close?"

"Five-thirty."

"I don't know if I can wait that long to see you again."

"I'm afraid you'll have to. My lunch break doesn't include leaving the Cottage."

"Darn."

She flashed him a cheeky grin. "We'll pick up where we left off by six. You're in charge of dinner."

"You should move in here. It will give us a lot more time to fool around."

"I don't think my folks would approve of me living in sin."

"I want to get married as soon as possible, at the Christmas Valley Inn."

"Perfect. By the time I see you tonight, we'll have a date figured out." She leaned down and kissed him goodbye, giving him a last gentle squeeze where it counted.

Sam reciprocated.

On the way to work, Tally called her parents. "Sam and I are getting married."

On speaker, they both cried, "Congratulations!"

"I need your help."

"You got it," her dad said.

"Tell us what you need," her mom said.

"We want to get married right away. Can you find out the next available date Christmas Valley Inn has open? Also, Sylvie told me once that Lily D'Arcy knows who to contact for quick weddings at the inn. Will you give her a call and get some appointments set up for me? I'd like them to all be on the same day, so it will make it easier to find someone to stand in for me at the Cottage."

"We're on it," Jean Barrow said.

"I'll take care of the guy end of things," Bryan promised.

"You're the best," Tally said.

"No," her mother replied. "You are. Somehow, you got over whatever it was that threw you off your feelings for Sam."

"I had a brain injury," Tally replied rather dryly. "That must have been what was wrong with me."

After a moment of startled silence, her parents laughed.

"Later, you guys."

At eleven a.m., Sam showed up at Gingerbread cottage with breakfast sandwiches he'd prepared at home. They got two coffees and ate in the storeroom while Zoë minded the store.

"I love you, Tally."

She smiled over the rim of her paper coffee cup. "I love you, too."

"Since I'm off work for a few days, I thought I could help out here. Griff says it's a no-brainer, as long as you smile pretty at the ladies."

He said it with such humor, Tally laughed. "I guess Griff oughta know, if anyone does. Bonnie says he draws women to the store in droves. Since you're at least as good-looking as he is, I expect business will be booming even more than it was on Saturday."

From then on, Sam spent most of his time talking to customers and carrying out their bags. He was a chick magnet, no doubt about it.

At three, her mother called. Tally took a moment to step away into the office to have the phone conversation.

"Here's what we've got," Jean said. "The inn is available next Sunday. I spoke with Stevie and Charley before I called them, because I'm certain you want them at the wedding. Turns out, they're not going to have Fruity-Cakes open on Sundays this season, so the date works perfectly. I have all your appointments scheduled for tomorrow. At nine o'clock, you'll meet with Lise Dennison at Katydid's for your dress. I'm assuming Sylvie will be your matron of honor, so I lined her up to meet us there. After that, it's Dress Up for your shoes and other accessories, then on to Carmen's Cakes to select your wedding cake, and a groom's cake, if Sam wants one. Then Blooms-a-Plenty for your flowers. Stella Falconio is standing by, in case you want your hair done prior to the ceremony." Her mother took a breath.

Bryan spoke up. "While you're taking care of all that, Sam and whoever his best man is will meet me at the tux shop."

"Sounds like you men are getting off easy," Tally teased.

"Dad and Sam will get the music part of things set up, and Sam already talked to Ryker about performing the ceremony."

"Yes, he told me, but wow, I'm exhausted just listening to you. Thanks so much for doing all this!"

"We're happy you asked for our help," Jean assured her. "Now, for the venue. Kris and Nick are happy to provide the food for a sit-down dinner, or you can have it catered from Delilah's Deliciousness. You and Sam figure out which you want, and I'll get the ball rolling."

"Let's go with catered," Tally said. "That way Kris and Nick can enjoy themselves."

"Good call. I have Delilah scheduled for your last stop tomorrow. Ask Sam to meet you at her shop to pick the menu."

"Uh, Sam's actually working with me at the Cottage until he's allowed to go back to work."

"Aw," Jean said, "isn't that sweet?"

"He's a great guy, Tally," Bryan agreed. "We're looking forward to welcoming him to our family."

"One last thing," her mother said. "We need an invitation list. You and Sam put your heads together tonight and get it to me in the morning, okay?"

"Sure." She and Sam would most likely be putting more than their heads together, but there should be some time between now and 9:00 a.m. to compile an invite list.

Tally reported everything her parents had accomplished to Sam over the Gingerbread Cottage cash register. He immediately called Grey Dixon and asked him to be his best man. Grey accepted and asked Sam to convey his apologies to Tally "for being a butthead."

After work, they went directly to Sam's house.

Tally lined up her sisters, Tessa and Jennie, and Zoë to work the shop the next day, so that was covered. She'd worried her sisters might have hurt feelings over not being her maids of honor, but they reminded her that they'd all made a pledge as girls *not* to ever be in each other's weddings. They assured her, they still held firm to that promise.

"I'd like sexy, romantic music," Tally informed Sam the next morning as they ate cereal standing up in his kitchen. "I'll give you a key to my place and you can look though my CD collection."

"And here I figured you for a pop girl," he said, giving her a leer.

"I'll pop you," she said, laughing.

Almost in unison, they set down their bowls and took the opportunity for a quickie.

By the time Tally rushed home to shower and change, she was almost late meeting her mother and Sylvie at Katydid's.

Tally wasn't a fashion maven, but she listened as Lise talked about the dresses she had on hand. "Don't worry that there's not much time before the wedding," Lise said. "If you find something you love, but it doesn't fit properly, I can make alterations."

Tally nodded, and began to peruse the selection. The third dress she landed on seemed like a good prospect, but it was the eighth dress she came to that won her heart. "This is it," she said to Lise.

"Oh, it's perfect for you!" Lise cried. "Let's get you into it."

"Tally, what are your colors?" Jean asked.

"This close to Christmas, how about red, green, and white?" Tally said.

While Tally got into the wedding gown, her mother and Sylvie made their selections. Jean chose a bing-cherry red cocktail dress and Sylvie found a luscious teal-green floor-length gown with an overblouse that accommodated her burgeoning belly nicely.

Tally stepped up on the platform in front of the mirror, so Lise could check the length. She hardly recognized herself in the mirror. "Wow, I have to admit, I never dreamed about getting married in a long white gown, but I'm in love with this one. It's amazing." The off-the-shoulder embroidered bodice, embellished with seed pearls, hugged her in ways she knew Sam would appreciate. And the flowing skirt…. "I feel like a fairy-tale princess."

From there, the mother, daughter, and daughter-in-law trio went appointment-to-appointment with the same success, including meeting Sam at the bakery, where he selected carrot cake for the groom's cake.

At the end of the day, Tally was exhausted. She called Sam to tell him she was going home to take a short nap before they met with Delilah to discuss catering.

"I'll join you," he said.

"Use your key to get in, in case I'm already asleep."

"I will. Did your mom think the guest list is okay?"

"She thinks its perfect. Probably most of the out-of-towners won't be able to come on such short notice, but if they do, there's still enough space for everyone. Mom and Sylvie will split the list and start calling tonight, even though Sylvie's sure everyone already knows, and they've all decided to leave their kids at home, so they can enjoy an evening out."

He laughed. "It'll be nice to see them, even *sans* kids."

"Bonnie and Griff will bring Rafe, for obvious reasons."

"Fine by me. I haven't seen the little tyke yet." His voice grew husky. "I can't wait for Sunday."

"Me, either." She lowered her voice to a purr. "Wake me up in a nice way."

He growled his response in a suggestive tone that set her hormones to fluttering. "You can count on it."

Chapter 29

Tally had her doubts that a wedding could be pulled together so quickly, but thanks to her mother, Sylvie, and Lily, here she was, at the top of the stairs of the beautifully decorated Christmas Valley Inn, ready to begin the next chapter of her life.

A week ago, she thought she'd be happy simply making love with Sam whenever they could work it into their schedules. But she'd come to realize that having sex with the man you loved was part of a much bigger package that included sharing small talk and important talk, emotions, worries, plans, concerns, and ideas.

He was already her best friend and her lover, and now he would also be her cohort in everything she did. He was her forever love and in some ways, that boggled her mind.

She hadn't listened to the playlist Sam and her dad had put together, but Sam had shared one bit of information with her. He'd borrowed the song Spense and Stevie had used at their wedding, for when she walked down the aisle. Though theirs would be a different version of the song, the lyrics, he said, were the important part.

When Tally heard "We've Only Just Begun" waft up the staircase, she knew she had nothing to worry about on the music front, and everything to look forward to with Sam.

As she entered the room, she only had eyes for him. He looked as if his tux had been tailor-made to fit him. He smiled and his eyes lit up when they met hers.

Arm-in-arm with her dad, she followed Sylvie down the short aisle. She handed her sister-in-law the bouquet of red gerberas, baby pearls, and white peonies and extended her hand to Sam. Somehow, he'd managed to get his casted wrist into the sleeves of his shirt and jacket. The cuff had been linked together with a rubberband, courtesy of her father.

Sam's fingers were warm and slightly rough. She could hardly wait to feel them roaming her body again.

She mouthed, *I love you.*

He smiled and mouthed back, *I love you, too.*

Ryker performed the ceremony, which they'd decided to keep traditional, with a few personalized touches. "I now pronounce you husband and wife."

Tally and Sam didn't wait for him to say, *You may kiss the bride*. They took it upon themselves to seal their vows with a really hot kiss. The guests applauded and a few whistles and *woots* could be heard from their ranks.

The couple pulled apart and grinned at their guests.

"We're in for a heckuva ride," Sam whispered in her ear.

"God, I hope so," she whispered back.

That made him laugh.

They posed for pictures and hugged everyone there, or at least Tally did. Sam shook hands with the men.

Once everyone was seated for dinner, Tally and Sam stood.

Tally said, "Sam and I would like to thank you for all your support, caring, and love over the past year. We can never repay your kindness, but at the same time, we want you to know we're here for you, if you ever need anything."

"That's right," Sam agreed. "It's because of all of you

that Tally and I are together now. We're blessed to be able to share the rest of our lives together, and we're blessed to call all of you our friends."

"We love you," Tally said.

Sam nodded. "We do."

Dinner was excellent, the wedding cake divine. Finally, Tally and Sam made their way upstairs to the honeymoon suite, which the Kringles always included as part of the wedding package.

Two zippers, several buttons, one cufflink, and one rubberband later, the two of them kissed, pressing against each other, naked as the day they were born.

"I can't believe I was so resistant to loving you," Tally said when he scooped her up into his powerful arms.

"I can't believe you were, either," he said with a grin. "I hear from the ladies who come into Gingerbread Cottage that I'm quite the 'hunky firefighter.'"

Tally grinned back. "Don't let it go to your head."

"Speaking of head…." He placed her gently on the bed.

Tally raised up on her elbows. "Thank you for the song."

"I looked up the lyrics, to make sure it said what I wanted to say."

"I loved it. It said what I wanted to say, too."

"I think we should do our talking a different way now." His eyes wandered to her breasts, then further south.

"I agree." She bit her bottom lip. "Do you think we'll make that baby we've been talking about?"

"I hope so." He tongued her breast. "You're going to be a great mom."

"And you'll be a terrific dad."

He chuckled. "We're our own mutual admiration society."

"Shut up and make love to me."

Without another word, Sam did just that.

The Christmas clock appeared on the antique table situated beneath the window. Totally at odds with its usual repertoire, the quiet strains of "We've Only Just Begun" provided the sweetest background music for their love-making.

The hands on the clock spun in a lazy fashion neither Tally nor Sam noticed.

They were way too busy noticing each other.

Author Note

Have you ever had a concussion? I have. I was in sixth grade at the time.

Everyone in the school was instructed to stay in the gym for lunch hour because it was *really* cold outside.

Instead, three of my friends and I got into our coats and went out to the farthest corner of the playground, where foot traffic had worn down the dirt. The depression had filled with snow, melted, refrozen, and made a terrific little ice pond to "skate" on.

Skip forward a few minutes. I fell and hit my head. The next thing I remember was being in the nurse's room. After that, I remember being at home in my bed, but not how I got there. I'm not sure how many days later I was allowed to go back to school, though once I was well, I was in trouble for not minding the rules.

Like Tally, I was impetuous as a youngster, and I probably shouldn't have gone outside that day, but it sure was fun sliding on the ice. It was also a lesson for me: every action has a consequence.

And that's enough about my childhood!

I'd like to thank my editor, Nancy Jankow, for her edits and suggestions that helped me make this the best book possible. As always, you rock, Nance!

I hope you enjoyed reading *Jingle Bell Clock*, because it certainly was fun to write. If you haven't read the other nine books in the series, please do give them a try, and look for two new books in November 2020.

Wishing you and yours a happy and merry Christmas!

Thank You!

Thank you so much for reading
JINGLE BELL CLOCK!
I'd love to hear what you think about it.
You can email me at **ann@annsimas.com**, or post
a comment on my **Ann Simas, Author** page on
Facebook. I hope you'll "like" me while you're
there, and if you are so inclined,
please leave a review on
Amazon.com, Goodreads.com,
or BookBub.com.

Just For Fun

If would like to submit a picture of yourself
reading this or any book by me, please send your
JPG to **ann@annsimas.com**
and I'll post it on my FAN page!

Available now, **HERE AND GONE**,
a thriller and a love story…
both will leave you breathless.

Turn the page for a preview.

HERE AND GONE

~ 1 ~

HANNAH MASON DIDN'T actually move into her new home under the cover of darkness, but she might as well have, for
all the subterfuge involved in her relocation.

That's what happened when you were a major front-
page headline in the local papers for months on end. Hannah called it crucifixion by journalism.

In the beginning, it had been difficult to crawl out of
bed and face the world. No one except her family got that
she was immersed in grief. Outside, vigilantism prevailed
and nothing short of burning her at the stake would have
satisfied those who had assumed the role of judge, jury,
and executioner.

If not for the diligence of that self-appointed lynch
mob, she might have crawled under the covers and given
up living altogether. Instead, being a woman of strong will
and determination, she forced herself to get up, get
dressed, and accomplish something every day, no matter
how small the task or how difficult the effort to climb out
of bed.

At first, that meant repairing the daily damage wrought
by those who persisted in leaving hateful graffiti on her
front door, or painted threats on her house. After almost a
year, the entrance to her home had so many coats of paint,
she gave up trying to conceal the messages and replaced
the door. Her brother-in-law installed a glass storm door
over that, which she locked every night, and cleaned with
a one-sided razor blade first thing almost every morning.

There wasn't a nasty negative word in the dictionary that hadn't been used against her.

Regardless of the absurd lies and conjectures the media invented, or how many times the police pounded her with the same questions they'd asked a dozen times before, or who the life insurance company sent to interrogate her, Hannah refused to cave into depression or desperation. She also worked hard not to succumb to the grief that consumed her from the inside out.

After the vile defacements had been obliterated each day, she forced herself to sit at her home-office work station. As a scientific illustrator, she'd taken on jobs from various publishers and authors and, by God, she'd complete them. She called them her rejuvenation pills. She also made time every day to work on the book she'd started for Jay. Getting lost in line drawings and colorations had turned out to be an unexpected salve against the sorrow she experienced for her lost little boy every hellacious day.

When she couldn't keep her eyes open any longer, she tumbled into bed, hoping, praying, for a dreamless slumber. If she was lucky, she only cried herself to sleep. If she wasn't, she had nightmares about how horrific it must have been for Jason and Jay, her husband and five-year-old son, out there on the vastness of the Pacific Ocean, in a sailboat, all alone, with no one to rescue them from drowning when the boat capsized.

She tried not to think about the creatures that lived and thrived beneath the water and how they'd react to the temptation of human flesh.

She tried not to think about the dying thoughts of the two people she cared about and loved more than her own life.

And most of all, she tried not to think about how she would face the rest of her life without them.

~ 2 ~

HANNAH THANKED GOD for the support of her siblings and their spouses. Without them, she might have gone crazy over the past two years, or given in to the haunting desire to join her husband and son in death.

Her sister Emily, six months pregnant, and her husband Craig, along with their brother Seth, and his wife Deena, had been instrumental in keeping Hannah's move and her final destination a secret. Much as she missed her parents, who had died before her marriage to Jason, she was grateful they hadn't lived to witness the lynch-mob mentality of the people they had called friends during their lifetime. The upside of them being in Heaven meant that her sweet little Jay had someone up there who loved him.

In conjunction with the move, Hannah had taken her illustrator *nom de plume* permanently, and backed it up with a legal name change. She clung to a wild hope that it would keep the media from tracking her down. For some obscure reason that she still didn't fully comprehend, they'd been so focused on denigrating and persecuting her with their words, they'd yet to discover her occupation. Both they and the police were under the mistaken assumption that she was nothing more than a rich housewife, bored with her husband and child. Even during the whole-house search, when the cops had torn out every drawer and emptied every closet, no one had ever questioned what she did with all the art supplies in her workroom.

The police hadn't found anything in the search, and why would they? They were completely misguided about her being either rich or bored. Yes, Jason had earned a big salary, but neither their joint personal bank account, nor their joint savings account had held any funds at his death. She'd opened a savings account under her illustrator name before she and Jason had married and all her payments and royalties were direct-deposited. If he'd had access, that account probably would have been emptied, too.

Hannah found it odd that the other accounts had been cleaned out down to a dollar each, but she had attributed it to Jason's strange behavior for the last year of his life. She figured he had a gambling problem, since he'd gone frequently to Las Vegas, or maybe he'd adopted an expensive drug habit. Certainly, he was doing something he shouldn't have been during the evening hours he claimed to be at work. Otherwise, wouldn't he have answered his phone, or been at his desk when she and Jay had dropped in to bring him a surprise dinner?

Her husband had a small life insurance policy through his work and another, larger one he'd bought personally. She hadn't spent one cent of that one, but had taken five thousand from the smaller one as a cushion and put the remaining balance in the safe deposit box. With frugal budgeting, she managed to live comfortably on the money generated from the sale of her house and what she earned from her illustrations. The five-thousand-dollar cushion had yet to be touched.

In the overall scheme of life, what she needed most wasn't money, but a snuggle and a sloppy kiss from her little boy, and unfortunately, that was never going to happen again.

Hannah tried to shake off the dark cloud hovering over her. This was a new place. She had a new life. The daytime was for work. Nighttime was for climbing into her big, lonely bed, where she could spend all the time she wanted thinking about Jason and Jay, missing them so much it left her in physical pain.

She especially agonized over Jay's loss. Jay, who would never have a chance to be a teenager or a man or have a family of his own. God, she hoped Jason had wrapped his arms around his son to comfort him when they were drowning. She couldn't bear the thought of her boy thrashing about in the water, scared out of his mind, maybe even crying out for her to save him.

Little puppy claws clickety-clacked over the hardwood

floors. Hannah forced the morbid thoughts from her mind and allowed herself to smile. She'd never had a dog before, and even though Bowie was still a pup, she was loving every minute of canine ownership. It would be even better when she got the golden retriever properly housebroken. He'd shown his intelligence already with his quick grasp of commands and his understanding of simple phrases, which gave her hope she wasn't simply cultivating a pipe dream about his smarts. "Ready to go outside?"

Bowie puppy-woofed.

Hannah grabbed her jacket. "Let's go."

Bowie raced to the door, but hadn't mastered the art of slowing down yet. He tried to put on his puppy brakes, but despite the belated effort, he slid the last five feet into the glass door. He yelped, as he always did, though he wasn't hurt, simply disgruntled.

Hannah laughed. These days, it was Bowie who kept her sane. What a horrible responsibility to thrust upon an innocent little puppy.

• • •

On Thanksgiving day, Hannah decorated a large Milk-Bone treat with a squirt of whipped cream from the Reddi-wip can in honor of Bowie's five-month birthday. For old-time's sake, she shot a squirt into her mouth, too. Even after all these years, her mother's warning still came through loud and clear…and it still made her smile. *Don't squirt whipped cream into your mouths from the can. We're civilized, you know!* When her mom wasn't looking, her dad would sneak into the kitchen and join her and Emily and Seth in what her brother had dubbed The Forbidden Whipped-Cream Adventure.

Hannah had carried on the tradition with her son. Her heart ached remembering how Jay had opened his little mouth in anticipation of receiving the Reddi-wip squirt. They'd giggle and giggle and Jason would scowl and tell them only pigs ate directly from the container. It was one of the many grudges her husband had come to nurture against her. For the life of her, Hannah had no idea what had caused the nice guy she'd married to morph into a mean malcontent who seemed to take pleasure from hurting her.

Bowie yipped to remind her she was still holding his treat. Every day, the yips and squeals out of his mouth were sounding more and more like real barks. Hannah glanced down and said, "Happy almost-half-year birthday, Bowie."

Bowie's butt, and consequently his tail, waggled about a hundred miles an hour in response.

"Sit."

Like the smart dog he was, Bowie sat.

Hannah leaned over and held the treat out for him to lick. That done, she handed over the Milk-Bone, which Bowie promptly took over by the patio door. He loved to lay in the winter sunlight.

She repeated the Milk-Bone treat for the next six days, until the Reddi-wip can was empty. Not bad. Four days for a human and her dog to polish off a can of whipped cream. "Don't get too used to this," she said, handing Bowie the biscuit. "Thanksgiving only comes once a year."

His tongue came out and licked his chops in anticipation.

Hannah laughed. "You don't even know what I'm saying, do you?"

In response, Bowie gave her one of his sweet smiles.

It was almost time for their morning walk around the property. The pup chewed contently on the biscuit, occasionally glancing at Hannah. Once it was devoured, he jumped up and ran over to her, then back to the door.

Hannah slipped into her snow boots, then pulled on her coat and gloves. "You're in for a new experience today, Bowie. It snowed last night."

He announced his excitement over the prospect of meeting snow by dancing a doggie two-step.

"When we get back, I'm going to build our first fire."

He smiled up at her.

"Let's go."

Bowie ran to the family room, then back toward the door, nearly managing to stop this time before he crashed into it.

Hannah chuckled. "You've almost got it, haven't you?" She reached down and patted his head.

The dog nuzzled her gloved hand.

She opened the door and Bowie shot outside. He got as far as the edge of the patio, which was dry because it had a cover, and came to a screeching halt. He lowered his muzzle to smell the snow, then lifted a paw and tentatively tested it. In the next instant, he backed away, turning to glance at Hannah as he did so.

She pulled the patio door closed and took off running into the yard. Twenty feet out, she turned to see what was keeping her dog. His butt was firmly planted on the cold concrete patio. "Chicken," Hannah said, laughing. "Bowie, come."

He stood, but other than that, made no move to follow the command.

"Bowie, come!"

This time he stepped gingerly into the snow, decided he liked it, and went down on his belly, licking the wet stuff as he crawled toward her.

"I'll go without you," Hannah threatened.

Bowie apparently didn't care. He rolled over and wriggled around on his back. Talk about a quick attitude conversion.

"Bowie, *come!*"

With obvious reluctance, he got up on all fours again and took a tentative step forward, and then another, and the next thing she knew, he was loping through the six-inch layer of snow, puppy-yipping for all he was worth.

Hannah laughed again and continued on toward the back of the property. Familiar with the route by now, she knew she wouldn't encounter anything beneath the snow to trip her up.

Bowie frolicked alongside her as she climbed the gentle slope. At the top of the hill, he went off to take care of business under his favorite tree. Five minutes later, he came back to her, cavorting like the puppy he still was, amusing her with his antics.

Half an hour later, they were back at the house. Hannah dried him off on the patio, including his wet little paws, before she let him inside. He thanked her with a generous lick.

She removed her boots outside the door, then took those and her coat to the mudroom, where she deposited her boots in the boot tray to drip dry. Her coat went on the last hook of the rack and her hat and gloves in a basket hanging from the first hook.

Not for the first time, Hannah marveled at the differences between beach living and mountain living. She'd never seen snow in person before moving to Fossil, so she and Bowie had that first experience in common. The snowman she'd built up on the hill, with Bowie's help, was no Frosty, but she'd have plenty of time to learn the proper way to make one.

Next on the agenda, breakfast. She put together a casserole using Italian sausage she'd browned and crumbled the day before, green chiles, grated cheddar, and eggs. While it baked, she put her boots back on and went out to get firewood. Whether it was ridiculous or not, she'd been waiting for the first snow to build her first fire. She found herself almost giddy with excitement.

After that, she walked out to the mailbox. Not that there would be anything other than bills, but she didn't want the mail carrier to report to authorities that she must be dead because her mailbox was stuffed full. Company, or anyone wearing a badge, was the last thing she wanted at her door.

Back inside, she made a pot of coffee, checked the timer on the oven, and went to her office to boot up her laptop. Emily sent her an email every morning, usually with a picture of her pregnant self. Today was no exception, if the little paperclip beside Em's name was any indication.

Hannah didn't eat while she was drawing, but she usually took her breakfast to her laptop to read the few emails she got and the day's news. She deleted three junk transmissions, read one from the editor she worked with at a publishing house, replied to a query from an author who was indie-publishing a children's book, and finally, it was time to read Emily's. She resisted looking at the attachments first. How much could her sister's belly have grown in one day, anyway?

Hannah,

I tried to call you last night and this morning, but your phone goes directly to voice mail. Please, please, please, since you insist on living in the wilderness, at least keep your phone on and charged if you're not going to check your email regularly!

Craig just returned from his East Coast trip. The way airlines are these days, with all the bumping and overbooking, he got bumped and had to take a different flight home, which necessitated changing planes in Denver to catch the flight home to San Diego.

Hannah shook her head. Emily always did take the long way around a story.

You may be wondering where all this is leading and all I can say is, I wanted you to understand how Craig came to be in Denver, but didn't stop to call or see you. He only had a 30-minute layover and he missed his connecting flight because the first leg was late. He tried to get another one, but at that point, they said they had nothing else available until morning. He was pissed, but he went out to catch a courtesy bus to a nearby hotel because he didn't want to sleep in the airport. He was waiting at the curb, when he got a call from the airline that they were going to get him on an 7:20 p.m. flight out, after all.

Before you read further, open the attachments I sent, then come back and read my second email.

em

Hannah's mouth twisted in a wry smile. Her sister could be such a drama queen. She put down her breakfast and used the mouse to open the first attachment.

Shock immobilized her. Instead of Emily's pregnant belly, up popped a picture of Jason. Although he sported a short beard, there was no mistaking him. Hannah enlarged the photo, then grabbed her magnifier to examine it more closely.

It was Jason, all right, unless he had an identical twin he'd never mentioned.

Or, it could be that she was losing her mind.

She jumped up and went to grab her cell phone, which was on the kitchen counter. She turned it on, on her way back to the workroom, where she opened the second attachment. Again, she stared at the photo, stunned.

Jason, Jay, and Sabine. How could that be? Jay looked older, which didn't compute with her memory of how he'd looked nearly two years before. Besides, how could that be, unless....

Unless he was still alive. Then, of course, he would be older. Had he lived, Jay would be almost seven now. And what was Sabine doing in the picture? She'd left San Diego a couple of weeks before Jason had taken Jay out on that fateful boat ride. Hannah had missed her friend terribly during those dark days when everyone else, including her neighbors, had treated her like a pariah.

She enlarged the photo and took the magnifier to it. There was no question. It was Jason with Jay and Sabine. Her mind was intact, but the facts in front of her didn't make sense.

She'd never seen Jason with a beard and though Jay was older, she still recognized him. Was this some good-intentioned effort on Craig's part to help make her feel better?

Her breakfast forgotten, Hannah hit speed dial for Emily. Instead of a greeting, she went straight to it. "What the hell is going on?"

· · ·

HERE AND GONE
Available worldwide in paperback or as an ebook at
amazon.com

Also available in paperback from
annsimas.com

About the Author

Ann Simas lives in Oregon, but she is a Colorado girl at heart, having grown up in the Rocky Mountains. An avid word-lover since childhood, she began to pen her first novel in high school. The author of 28 novels, one novella, and seven short stories, she particularly enjoys writing books that are cross-genre—a mix of mystery/thriller/suspense, with a love story and paranormal or supernatural elements.

In addition to being a three-time Romance Writers of America Golden Heart Finalist, Ann is also an award-winning watercolorist and budding photographer who enjoys needlework and gardening in her spare time. She is her family's "genealogist" and has been blessed with the opportunity to conduct first-hand research in Italy for both her writing and her family tree. The genealogy research from century's-old documents, written in Italian, has been a supreme but gratifying and exciting challenge for her.

Contact the author via:
Magic Moon Press
POB 41634
Eugene, OR 97404-0386
or at **ann@annsimas.com**

Or visit:
annsimas.com *and*
Ann Simas, Author on Facebook
Ann Simas on BookBub.com

Ann's books are available worldwide at
amazon.com

Made in the USA
Columbia, SC
05 November 2022

70517381R00136